Joseph Jacobs, Giovanni Boccaccio

Tales from Boccaccio

Joseph Jacobs, Giovanni Boccaccio

Tales from Boccaccio

ISBN/EAN: 9783337070632

Printed in Europe, USA, Canada, Australia, Japan

Cover: Foto ©Andreas Hilbeck / pixelio.de

More available books at **www.hansebooks.com**

TALES
from
BOCCACCIO

GEORGE · ALLEN · PUBLISHER · LONDON · 156 · CHARING · CROSS · ROAD · RUSKIN · HOUSE ·

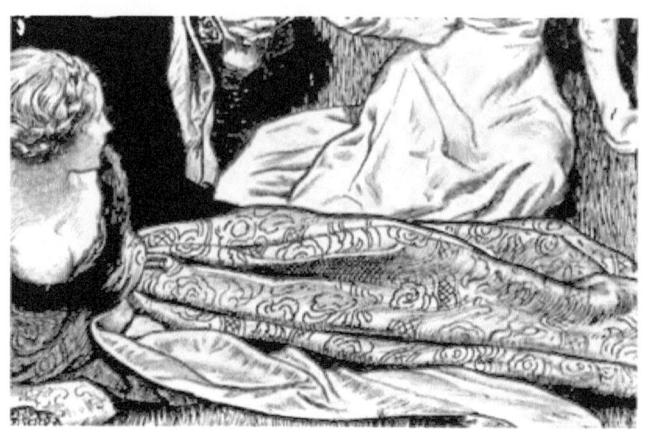

TALES
from
BOCCACCIO

done into
English
by
JOSEPH
JACOBS
illvstrated
by
BYAM
SHAW

1899

LONDON·GEORGE·ALLEN·RVSKIN·HOVSE

CONTENTS

LIST OF ILLUSTRATIONS

INTRODUCTION

IT is unfortunate that Boccaccio's reputation
generally relegates him to the top shelves,
whence he is only supposed to be removed
furtively and at moments of weakness.
That the *Decamerone* contains tales which are more
broad than they are long it would be idle to deny.
In Boccaccio's days such tales used to be put down
on paper, and published unblushingly, instead of
being confined to the oral tradition of smoking-
rooms, or to "limited editions" of a thousand
copies, supposed to be for private circulation only,
but really as accessible as a prayer-book or a direc-
tory. Yet after all, there are only twenty-eight of
the hundred tales of the *Decamerone* which need
fall under the ban of the censor, and the remaining
seventy-two have never been surpassed for the

mastery with which they touch all the chords of human feeling and passion, from the lightest to the most tragic.

It is, indeed, in his command of the sterner passions that move the human breast that Boccaccio has shown himself the greatest master. There is never a word wasted ; he selects with consummate artistry just those acts and words of the chief actors that are best suited to produce the καθάρσις. He wrote at the dawn of modern literature, yet none has ever bettered, if any has ever equalled him in the art of putting narrative shortly but well. He was endowed with all the qualifications of the narrative artist—wit, natural conversation, exquisite choice of incident, easy flow of dialogue and event, are his at their highest degree ; yet, because he is sometimes coarse, his masterpiece is never referred to, and only consulted stealthily. Truly virtue is its own punishment. Not that he has been neglected by real readers, and especially by those virile thinkers who held up the mirror to Nature on the stage.

Shakespeare knew and used him, so did Molière ; and his situations, not excluding those of which we ought to profess ignorance, have ruled the drama ever since it developed out of the Morality stage. Nor is the indebtedness of the drama to him entirely on account of the lighter elements. Tancred and Griselda found their way on the boards, where Masetto and Alibech never followed them. In the prose literature of Italy, which he practically founded, his method dominated for at least three centuries, and we get the name, if not the method, of the novel from the school which he brought into being.[1]

In opposition, or at least contrast, to the *Divina Commedia*, Boccaccio has given us the *Commedia Umana*, filled with as many figures, and as well drawn in their way, as that of Balzac. Yet it is probable that he himself regarded the hundred sketches of the *Decamerone* as merely slight things,

[1] I have given in the Introduction to my edition of Paynter's "Palace of Pleasure"—the story-store of Elizabethan drama—some account of the Italian *novella*.

thrown off in the intervals of the real work of his life. His was the age of encyclopædias, and it was with his Genealogy of the Gods and biographies of celebrated women, both written in Latin, that Boccaccio would probably have claimed affinity with the Muses, whom he first learned to worship (according to Villani) at Virgil's grave. It is somewhat curious to reflect also that at the somewhat mature age of forty-eight he became converted and pious, but does not seem to have taken any steps to remove the *Decamerone* from circulation. Beside all his other claims to attention, he has that of being the first of modern men to study Homer in the original, and the first of Italians to comment on Dante. Truly in the sixty-two years of his life (1313–1375) he passed through many phases, and in all of them he had an eye to the vital qualities of human life.

Nowhere has he shown this characteristic more clearly than in the four tales selected from the *Decamerone* in this volume. They all deal with the more serious aspect of Boccaccio's work, and thus to some extent give only one side of his genius. It is that side which is less thought of in connection with him, and perhaps may come with the greater force and revelation to those who associate his name solely with smoking - room stories. Here, almost for the first time in Europe, did a writer in the vernacular attempt in prose tragic themes. Only one of the stories before us deals with the height of Boccaccio's argument. The fifth novel of the fourth day, known in the original as *Lisabetta*, but retaining here the title of *Isabella*, acclimatised in England by Keats, was probably based on some real occurrence in the land of high passions, but Boccaccio deals with his theme with the most effective conciseness, laying no exaggerated stress either on the dastardly vengeance of the brothers, or the piteous grief of his heroine. All is told simply and naturally, and the result is much more effective than the most ranting elaboration.

The story that opens our volume has become known throughout Europe by folk-song and

folk-play, till the patient Grissel has become a by-
word. The wish of the men who heard the story
may have been father to its popularity. If Grissel
were to be regarded as a possible creation, she must
be an Old Woman indeed. The story runs the
older idea of a woman's place in the household to
its logical and most brutal end. Only in folk-lore
do we find any counterpart to Griselda's story, and
there it is suspected that the Russian folk-tale
given by De Gubernatis in his *Zoological Mythology*
was derived indirectly from Boccaccio's tale itself.
Yet in one of the Lays of Marie de France there
is an incident not altogether unlike our story, in
which the people of Brittany beg their Count to
put aside Fraisne, and to take Coudre, her sister.
The nearest parallel, however, as might have been
expected, is to be found in the despotic East,
which (so the ladies say) has failed to progress
because it took so low a view of woman. In
Miss Stokes' Indian fairy tales there is a story of
a king who threatens to kill any child of his that
cries, and then to kill the mother if she cries

because her child is killed. He does this twice, and it is only with the third mother that he finds the Indian "patient Grissel."

It is hard for a Western to be patient with patient Grissel. What seems to Boccaccio the highest merit strikes a modern as little less than criminal, yet few of Boccaccio's women show such want of spirit as Griselda does, and one cannot but suspect that Boccaccio had before him some folk-tale or other, rather than any experience of real life in Italy. Yet it is characteristic that Petrarch, his friend, chose this particular tale to put into Latin, and it is from Petrarch rather than Boccaccio that Chaucer derives his treatment of the subject.

But allowing for the change of opinion about woman's position in life, one cannot deny the artistry with which Boccaccio presents his theme. From the somewhat brutal speech of the Count at the beginning to the tender prayer of Griselda towards the end—that he may not treat the new wife as he had treated her—every touch is effective,

and increases our admiration for the heroine, if
only we could consider her conduct natural.   If
one could accept the Oriental ideal of women,
Griselda would indeed answer to that ideal.

A sort of companion-picture on the man's side
is afforded by the story of Sir Federigo and his
hawk, also included in this volume.   Here the
pundits like Dr. M. Landau have sought for
analogues in folk-tale and Eastern story.   There
is indeed something Buddhistic in the supreme
sacrifice of Federigo.   The well-known story of
Buddha offering himself as a meal for a hungry
tiger—in some forms of the tale merely to satisfy
the tiger's hunger, in others to relieve those who
might be victims—is scarcely more striking as an
example of self-sacrifice than Federigo's giving up
the hawk, which was not alone his only amuse-
ment, but seemingly his only means of obtaining
food.   One of the Meyrick girls in *Daniel Deronda*
objects that Buddha himself might have been
hungry at the time, and certainly one feels a
certain want of sympathy with what seems an

unnecessary sacrifice ; but it is just with those sublime extravagances of feeling that the artist in narrative produces his finest effects, and one cannot wonder at the youthful Tennyson being led to translate *The Falcon* into his pellucid verse. German folk-lore gives a religious turn to the story in the tale told by Haltrich, in which a shepherd gives his solitary pet lamb for a meal to Christ and St. Peter warming themselves in his house, but with the usual consequence of receiving a whole flock instead.

Nowhere does Boccaccio's skill in tale-telling show to better advantage than in the admirable story of *Saladin*, included in this volume. In a romance of an earlier contemporary of Boccaccio's, named Busone da Gubbio, the main incident of the tale is told as having really occurred to Saladin, who, according to Busone, met in Spain with a knight named Hugo di Moncaro, who in order to force the Sultan to accept his hospitality, loosed the nails from his horses' shoes, and treated him right worthily, though he was ignorant of his

b

station.   Afterwards, during the Crusades, he fell
into Saladin's power, who set him and his companions free, and sent him home with ten thousand
gold pieces.   From this simple anecdote Boccaccio
has developed a tale full of interest and incident.
The picture of well-bred courtesy displayed in
Torello's reception of the unknown Oriental
stranger is full of subtle touches that give it real
vitality in our minds.   The care of Torello's wife
to provide the strangers with fine linen, because as
merchants they were probably used to that somewhat rare luxury, adds the final touch.   When
we are transported to the East, a change comes
over the character of the story, which makes it
almost unique among the tales of the *Decamerone*.
We seem to be reading some incident in the
Thousand and One Nights, with the quick change
of status, the grandiose hospitality and generosity
of the Sultan, and finally the transformation scene
at the end, reminding one of Nour-ed-Din and the
Fair Persian.   But a few years after Boccaccio told
the tale, Chaucer was to leave half told the tale

in which a magic horse conveys the hero of the
Squire's Tale through the air. Similar stories are
told of saints and sinners in the West, but they
are mostly after contact with the East, and enabled
the Occidentals to be acquainted with the aërial
locomotion of Asia. One cannot but think that
Boccaccio must have had some folk-tale before him,
since the recognition by a ring is so frequent an
incident in such narrations. The opportune arrival
of Torello on the very marriage day of his wife
is also a folk trait, found in many a fairy story
and ballad : " Young Lochinvar " is one of the
most familiar instances, though Scott probably
had " Childe Horn " in memory.

But it is the skill with which Boccaccio has
woven together these incidents from the stories
of the folk which calls for our attention here.
Notice, for example, the subtle change from the
contemptuous " thou " to the respectful " you,"
when Saladin has his first talk with Torello at
Alexandria. Observe, too, the gracious compli-
ment which Saladin pays to Torello's wife—

the more marked as coming from a follower of
Islam. The dramatic way, too, in which the dis-
covery of Torello in the church is told interests
of itself, and gets over the difficulty of the super-
natural machinery; and then the combined courtesy
and wit with which Torello greets the disappointed
bridegroom, who would have robbed him of his
wife, is all in the best style of narrative art.

The triumph is all the more marked, since one
can clearly trace in the language of the story the
influence of the periodic Latin in which most lite-
rary men were accustomed to make their effects.
Italian with Dante had not yet obtained true ease ;
there was a certain stiffness in the movement of
the sentences, which required a master like Boccaccio to overcome. In the lighter stories, so far
as can be observed, Boccaccio breaks through, to
some extent, the more formal collocation of sentences derived from Latin, but in the more
serious attempts exemplified in this volume he is
clearly aiming at showing that Italian can produce as much effect as the more classical tongue.

Notwithstanding this somewhat artificial method of treating his native language, he has succeeded in putting his points neatly and effectively, and with the greatest economy of word-play. If he is somewhat stiff in his narration, he is at any rate full of ease in his conversations, where it would have been impossible for him to have kept the Latin formation of sentences.

This combination of colloquial ease in conversation and periodic formation in the surrounding narration, renders the translator's task more than ordinarily difficult in the case of these tales. For two of them I have had the advantage of being able to consult Mr. John Payne's admirable version, which only errs in a somewhat unnecessary amount of archaism. It would, of course, be poor art to transfer Boccaccio into the ordinary speech of to-day, but there is a limit to the amount of quaintness which may be legitimately imported into a translation of a mediæval story, and I am inclined to think that Mr. Payne at times oversteps the limit. The ideal translation would produce the same effect in the reader's mind nowadays as the original produced on the ordinary Italian in the fourteenth century. It is, of course, impossible to attain such an ideal, for the simple reason that some of Boccaccio's terms and thoughts are in themselves archaic, and in such cases a due use of archaisms is justifiable. In particular, nothing can be more subtle, as I have observed, than the use Boccaccio makes of the second singular and plural, and even at the risk of appearing too formal, I have throughout retained the contrast. It must be left to the reader to judge how far I have succeeded in the difficult task of being literal, and at the same time easeful, in reproducing the great Italian's words.

However ineffective my version may be, it cannot altogether fail to represent to the English reader some of the skill with which Boccaccio has told his tales. The lightness of touch, the economy of incident, the naturalness of conversation, cannot have been altogether obscured ; and all this without a single model before him. Like the French

general, Boccaccio might say, " *Je suis ancêtre.*"
He is the father of all the tale-tellers of Europe
since his time—whether grave or gay. Usually
his name is only associated with the brighter
forms of narration, but the stories before us will
indicate that he has as much command over the
deeper feelings and the more moving passions, as
he has over the more humorous and lighter sides
of human nature. He is indeed the supreme
master of the *conte*.

JOSEPH JACOBS.

CALIFORNIA

Now this Marquis spent his time in nothing other than
hawking and hunting

Here beginneth
the Tale of
Griselda

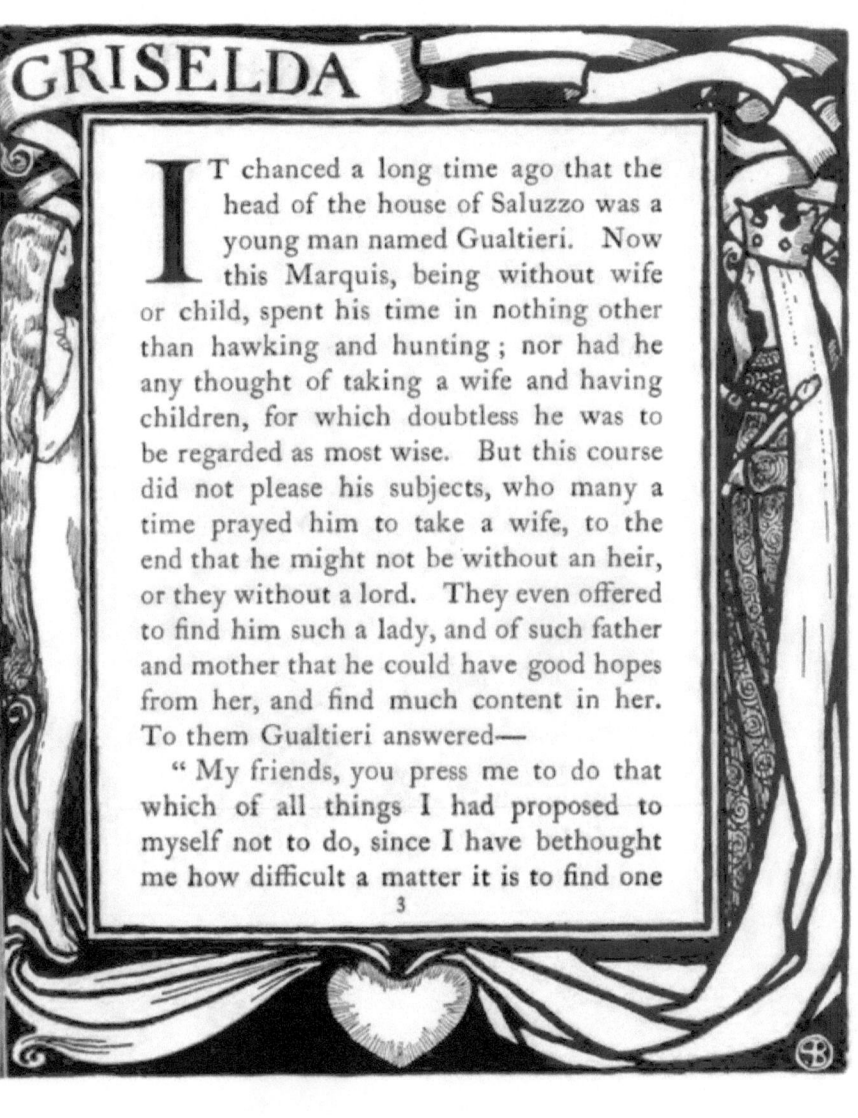

GRISELDA

IT chanced a long time ago that the head of the house of Saluzzo was a young man named Gualtieri. Now this Marquis, being without wife or child, spent his time in nothing other than hawking and hunting; nor had he any thought of taking a wife and having children, for which doubtless he was to be regarded as most wise. But this course did not please his subjects, who many a time prayed him to take a wife, to the end that he might not be without an heir, or they without a lord. They even offered to find him such a lady, and of such father and mother that he could have good hopes from her, and find much content in her. To them Gualtieri answered—

"My friends, you press me to do that which of all things I had proposed to myself not to do, since I have bethought me how difficult a matter it is to find one

3

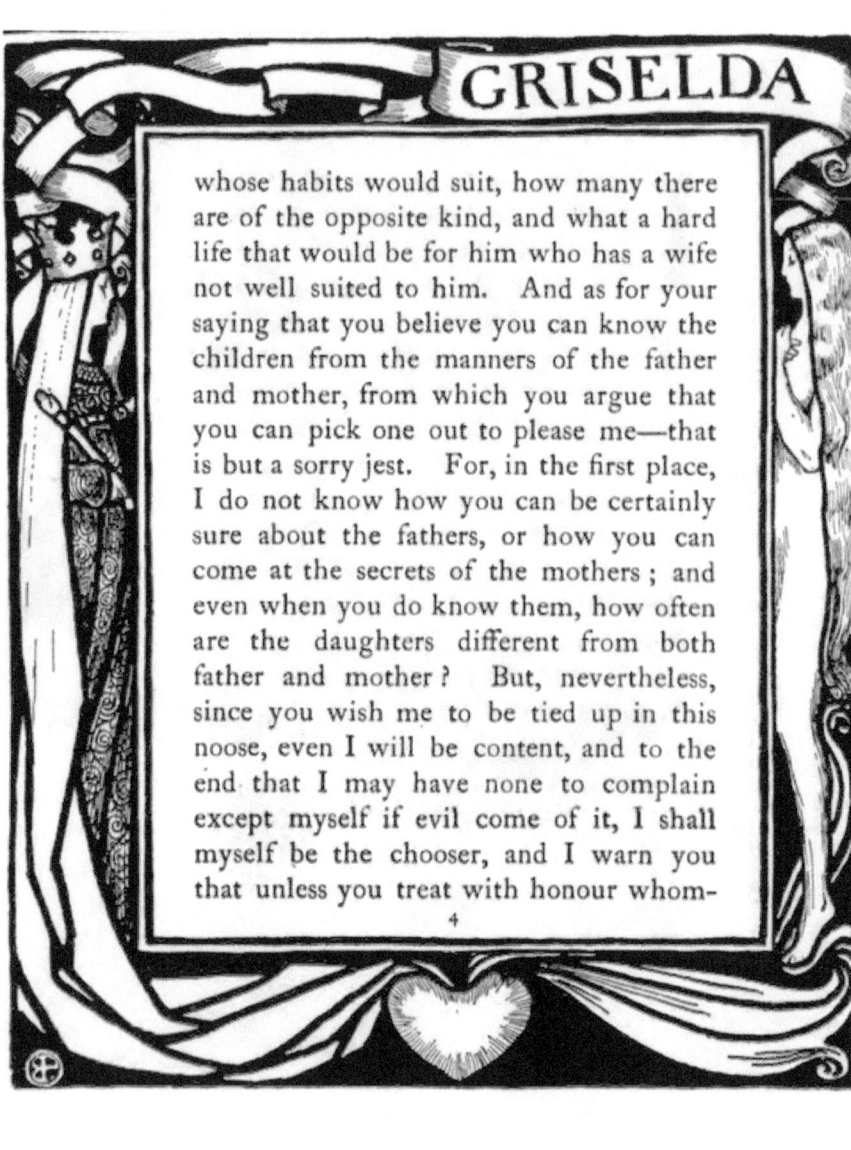

whose habits would suit, how many there are of the opposite kind, and what a hard life that would be for him who has a wife not well suited to him. And as for your saying that you believe you can know the children from the manners of the father and mother, from which you argue that you can pick one out to please me—that is but a sorry jest. For, in the first place, I do not know how you can be certainly sure about the fathers, or how you can come at the secrets of the mothers; and even when you do know them, how often are the daughters different from both father and mother? But, nevertheless, since you wish me to be tied up in this noose, even I will be content, and to the end that I may have none to complain except myself if evil come of it, I shall myself be the chooser, and I warn you that unless you treat with honour whom-

4

But this course did not please his subjects

CALIFORNIA.

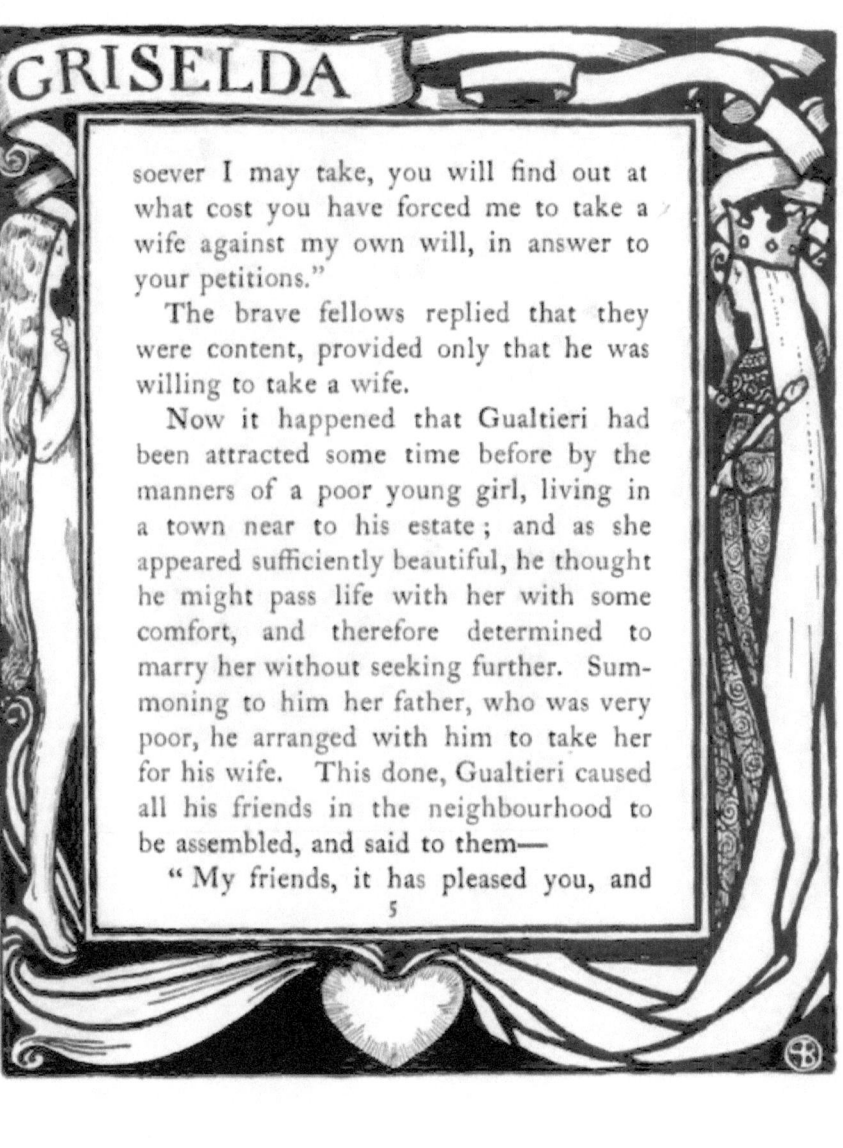

soever I may take, you will find out at what cost you have forced me to take a wife against my own will, in answer to your petitions."

The brave fellows replied that they were content, provided only that he was willing to take a wife.

Now it happened that Gualtieri had been attracted some time before by the manners of a poor young girl, living in a town near to his estate; and as she appeared sufficiently beautiful, he thought he might pass life with her with some comfort, and therefore determined to marry her without seeking further. Summoning to him her father, who was very poor, he arranged with him to take her for his wife. This done, Gualtieri caused all his friends in the neighbourhood to be assembled, and said to them—

"My friends, it has pleased you, and

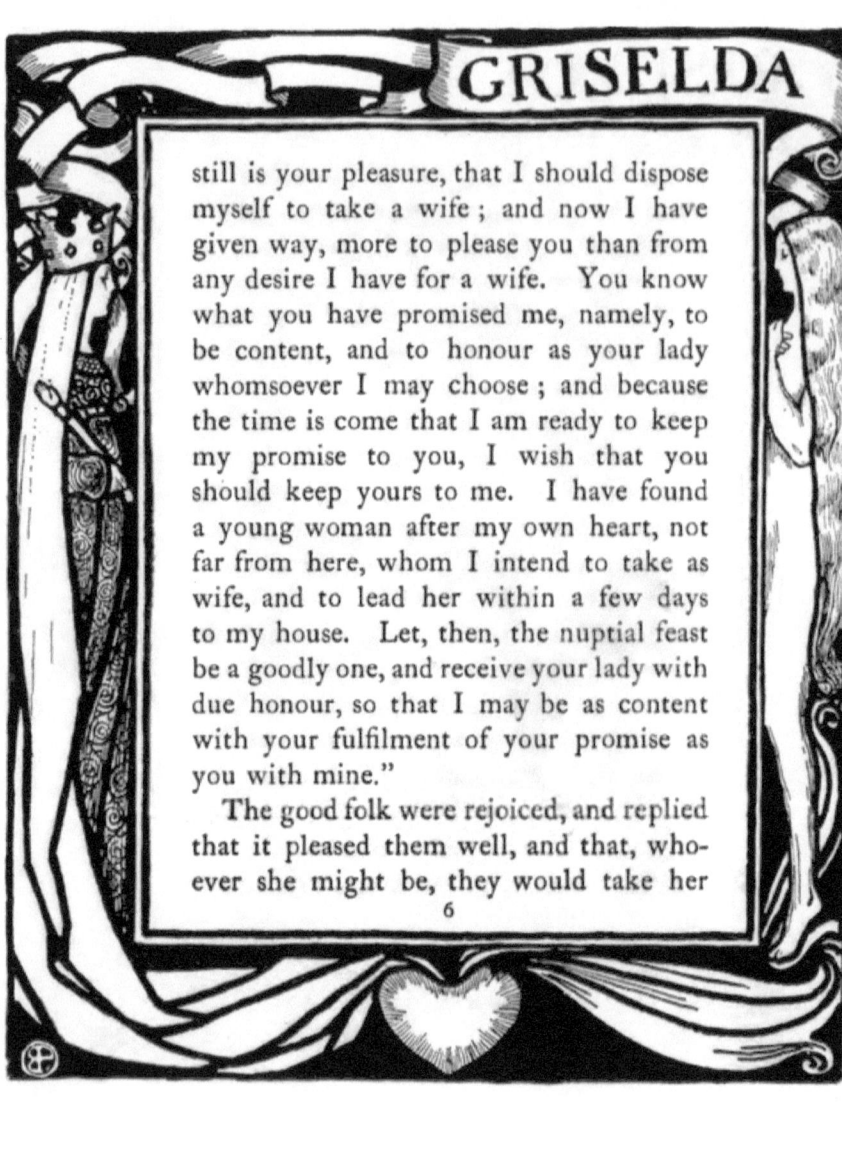

still is your pleasure, that I should dispose myself to take a wife; and now I have given way, more to please you than from any desire I have for a wife. You know what you have promised me, namely, to be content, and to honour as your lady whomsoever I may choose; and because the time is come that I am ready to keep my promise to you, I wish that you should keep yours to me. I have found a young woman after my own heart, not far from here, whom I intend to take as wife, and to lead her within a few days to my house. Let, then, the nuptial feast be a goodly one, and receive your lady with due honour, so that I may be as content with your fulfilment of your promise as you with mine."

The good folk were rejoiced, and replied that it pleased them well, and that, whoever she might be, they would take her

6

for their lady, and honour her in all things as such. And afterwards they all put themselves to much pains to make the day grand and joyful, and the same did Gualtieri. He let prepare the bridal on a grand scale, and invited to it many of his friends and relatives, and many great folk from round about ; and he caused most rich and costly robes to be prepared from the model of a young woman who resembled in person the maiden whom he proposed to marry ; and besides this, prepared girdles and rings, and a rich and beautiful crown, and everything that beseemed a new bride. And when the day came which he had fixed for the nuptials, Gualtieri at the third hour mounted his horse, and so did all those who had come to him to do him honour. And everything being prepared, he said to them, "My lords, it is time to go for the new bride," and leading the way with all his company, he arrived at the village; and near to the house of her father he found the damsel, who was just returned from drawing water in great haste from the well, intending to go afterwards with other women to see the bride of Gualtieri arrive.

Now when Gualtieri saw her, he called her by her name, that is, Griselda, asking where her father was. She modestly replied, "My lord, he is at home." Thereupon Gualtieri dismounted, and commanding to all men that they should await him, he entered alone into the poor dwelling, where he found her father, whose name was Giannucolo, and said to him—

"I am come to wed Griselda; but first of all I desire to know from her certain things in thy presence;" and there-

8

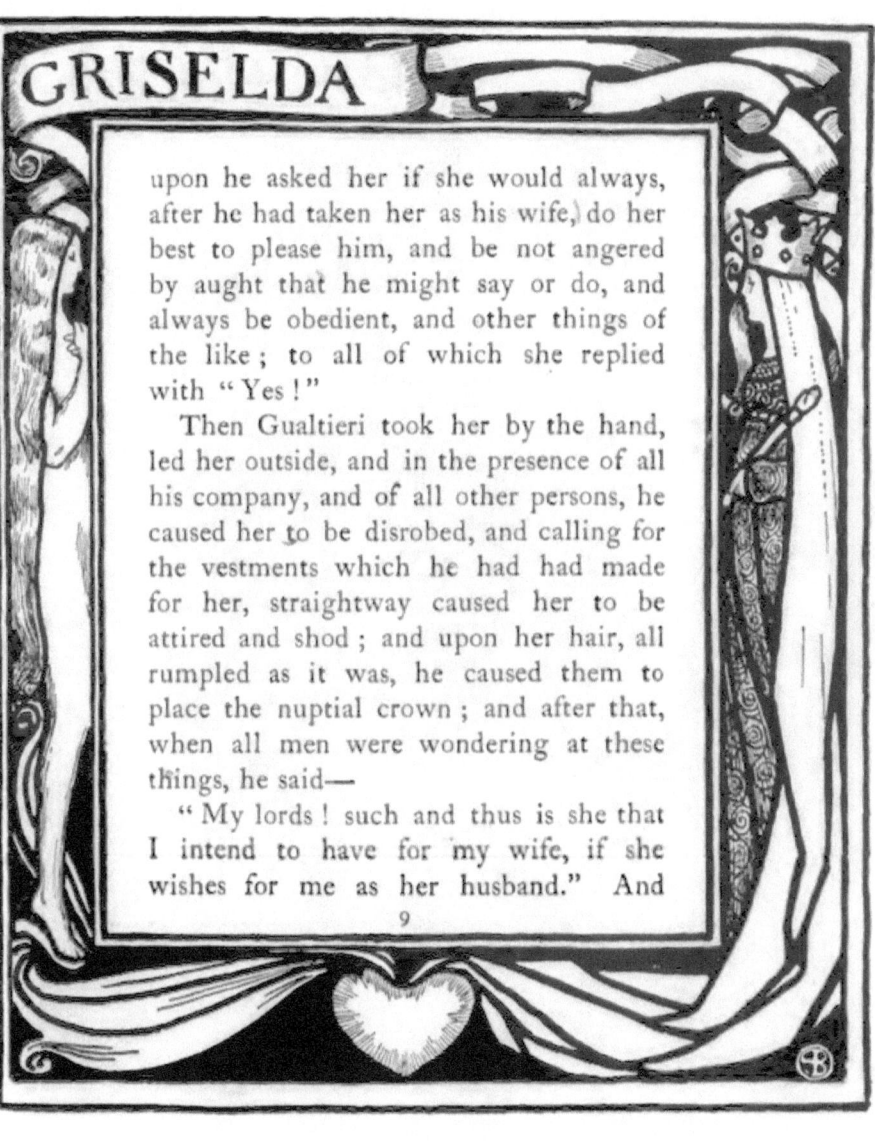

upon he asked her if she would always, after he had taken her as his wife, do her best to please him, and be not angered by aught that he might say or do, and always be obedient, and other things of the like ; to all of which she replied with " Yes !"

Then Gualtieri took her by the hand, led her outside, and in the presence of all his company, and of all other persons, he caused her to be disrobed, and calling for the vestments which he had had made for her, straightway caused her to be attired and shod ; and upon her hair, all rumpled as it was, he caused them to place the nuptial crown ; and after that, when all men were wondering at these things, he said—

" My lords ! such and thus is she that I intend to have for my wife, if she wishes for me as her husband." And

9

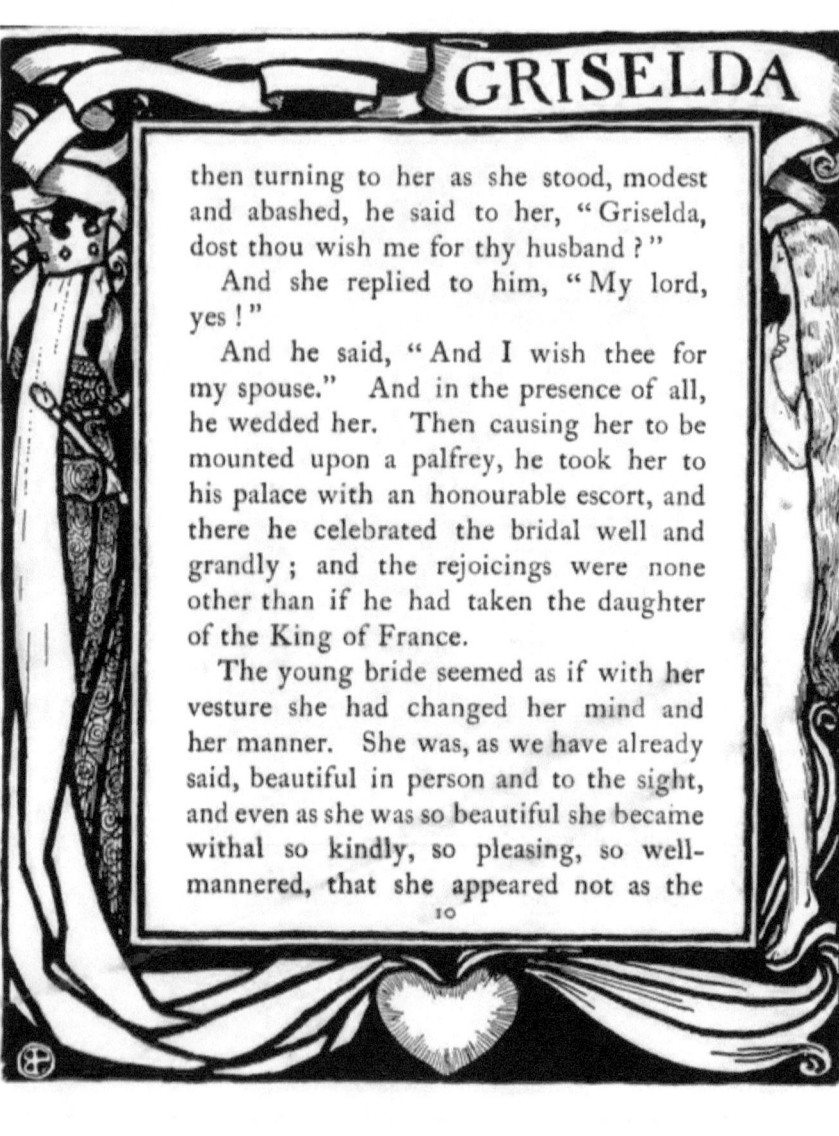

then turning to her as she stood, modest and abashed, he said to her, "Griselda, dost thou wish me for thy husband?"

And she replied to him, "My lord, yes!"

And he said, "And I wish thee for my spouse." And in the presence of all, he wedded her. Then causing her to be mounted upon a palfrey, he took her to his palace with an honourable escort, and there he celebrated the bridal well and grandly; and the rejoicings were none other than if he had taken the daughter of the King of France.

The young bride seemed as if with her vesture she had changed her mind and her manner. She was, as we have already said, beautiful in person and to the sight, and even as she was so beautiful she became withal so kindly, so pleasing, so well-mannered, that she appeared not as the

10

daughter of Giannucolo and a shepherdess, but of the stock of some noble signor ; in such wise that she made all marvel who had known her before. Beyond that, she was so obedient to her husband, and so submissive, that he thought himself the most satisfied man in the world. And likewise towards her husband's subjects she was so gracious and so benign, that there was none that did not love and honour her. All prayed heartily for her health and prosperity, and for her advancement. And whereas they used to say that Gualtieri had acted with little wisdom in taking her for his wife, they now said that he was the wisest and subtlest man in the world, for that none ever but he could have recognised her thorough virtues under her poor dress and village costume. In short, not alone in his own marquisate, but throughout the

country, before much time was passed
she caused all men to speak of her exceeding worth and her good works ; and
if anything was said against her husband
when she had been wedded by him, it
was now all the other way. She had not
remained long with Gualtieri before she
proved with child, and in due time bore
a daughter, at which Gualtieri made a
great feast.

But a short time after this a new
thought entered his mind, namely, to
prove her patience by long trials and intolerable suffering. At first he ill-used
her only with words, showing himself
angered, and declaring that his subjects
were ill content with her for her low
condition, and especially when they saw
that she was bearing children, and in
their grief at the daughter she had already
borne they did naught but murmur. And

when the lady heard these words, without changing her countenance or behaviour in any manner, she answered—

"My lord, do with me whatever thou dost think best for thy honour and consolation, for I shall be content with all, seeing that I know that I am the least of all thine, and that I was not worthy of that honour to the which thou hast by thy courtesy raised me."

This reply was very dear to Gualtieri, proving that she was in no manner puffed up by pride at the honour which he or others had done to her.

A short time after, having in general words told his wife that his subjects could not bear the daughter she had borne, having instructed one of his familiars, he sent him to her with a very grievous countenance, and said—

"Madam, if I am not to die, it behoves

13

me to do that which my lord has commanded me. He has ordered me that I
should take your little girl, and that I . . ."
He said no more.

The lady, hearing these words, and
seeing the countenance of the familiar,
and remembering her husband's words,
understood that it had been ordered him
to kill the little child. But at once she
took it out of the little cradle, and kiss-
ing it and blessing it as if she felt great
grief in her heart, without changing
countenance placed it in the arms of the
familiar, and said—

"Take her, and do with her entirely
what thy and my lord hath commanded ;
only do not leave her where the beasts
and birds may devour her, unless he hath
commanded that too to thee."

The familiar took the little girl, and
let Gualtieri know what the lady had said

14

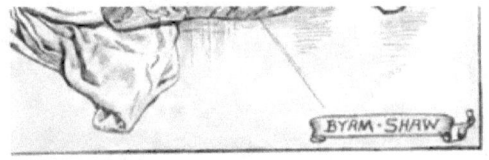

familiar took the little girl.

to him, and he, marvelling much at her
constancy, sent him with the child to one
of his relatives at Bologna, begging her,
without saying whose child she was, to
rear her up and train her diligently.

It happened shortly afterwards that the
lady was again with child, and at the due
time bore a male child that was most
dear to Gualtieri. But not satisfied with
that which he had done, he treated the
lady with still greater harshness, and
with seeming anger said to her one
day—

"Lady, since thou hast brought me
this male child, in nowise can I live
with these men of mine, so harshly do
they complain that a grandson of Giannucolo shall become their lord after me,
and it has come to this, that if I am not
to be hunted from my own land, I must
do with this what I did the time before,

and after that leave thee and take another
wife."

The lady heard him with patient mind,
and made no other reply than this—

" My lord, think only of contenting
thyself, and of satisfying thy pleasure,
and have no other thought of me, since
naught is dear to me except in so far as I
can see it pleases thee."

Not many days afterwards, Gualtieri,
in the same manner as he had sent for
the girl, sent for the boy, and in like wise
pretending that he had caused him to be
killed, sent him to be reared at Bologna,
as he had sent the little girl. And at this
the lady looked nor said otherwise than
she had done with her daughter, at which
Gualtieri marvelled greatly, and to himself declared that no other woman could
have done what she had done. And if it
had not been that she had been most
16

loving to the children while that pleased him, he would have thought that she had done this through not caring for them any longer, whereas he knew otherwise.

His subjects, thinking that he had caused the children to be slain, blamed him much, and considered him a cruel man, and had the greatest compassion for the lady. But she said naught to the ladies who condoled with her at her children thus dead, but that it was not hers but his pleasure who had begat them.

Several years having passed since the birth of his daughter, it seemed time to Gualtieri to make the last proof of her patience. He said to many of his men, he could no longer bear to have Griselda for wife, that he recognised that he had done a wicked and youthful thing when he had taken her, and since he could procure a dispensation from the Pope, he intended to take another wife and let Griselda go : for which he was much blamed by many good men, but he made no answer to them except that the thing suited him. The lady, hearing these things, and fearing she must expect to return to her father's house, and perhaps to guard the sheep as she had done formerly, while seeing another lady possess him to whom she had given all her thoughts, grieved greatly to herself; but as she had borne the other mischances of fortune, so she prepared herself with a firm countenance to bear this new one.

Not long afterwards, Gualtieri caused forged letters to come from Rome, and showed them to his subjects, in which the Pope granted dispensation for him to take another wife than Griselda, and let her go. And thereupon causing her to come before him, in the presence of many he said to her—

"Lady, by the dispensation granted me by the Pope, I can take another wife and let thee go. Since my forebears have been great gentlemen and lords of this country, whereas thine have always been work-men, I intend that thou shalt no longer be spouse of mine, but that thou shalt return to the house of Giannucolo with the dowry that thou broughtest to me ; and I can then take unto myself another, found to be more suitable for me."

The lady, hearing these words not with-out the greatest dismay, contrary to the wont of women, kept back her tears, and replied—

"My lord, I always knew that my lowliness of condition did not in aught accord with your nobility, and in that I have been placed in the same condition with you, I owe that to you and to God; nor have I ever held it as being given to me, but only as lent. Be pleased, therefore, to take it back, as it pleases me to please you and return it. Behold your ring, with which you espoused me: take it! You command that I take back with me the dowry which I brought: to do that needs no treasure of yours, or any purse of mine; it needs not a sumpter mule to carry it, nor have I forgotten that you took me without apparel. If you judge it honourable that that body which has borne you two children shall be seen by all, I will go unapparelled; but I pray you, in recompense for my maidenhood, which I brought hither and cannot carry back, that you be pleased that I may carry one smock alone in addition to my dowry."

Gualtieri, though he would sooner have

wept than do aught else, stood with harsh visage and said—

"One smock only mayest thou carry." And many of those around him prayed that he would give her one dress, that she might not be seen in that state who had been his wife for thirteen years and more, that she should go forth from his house thus poorly and contemptuously, if she were to go forth in her smock alone. But in vain were the prayers, so that the lady, in her smock and barefoot, without aught on her head, commended him to God and went forth from the house, and returned to her father with the tears and plaints of all those who saw her.

Giannucolo, who had never been able to believe that it could be true that Gualtieri would keep his daughter as his wife, and had been always expecting this, had kept the rags which were taken off

on the morning that Gualtieri had wedded
her. Wherefore he brought them out,
and she put them on again, and devoted
herself to the menial tasks of her father's
house, as she had been accustomed, bearing with brave mind the fierce assaults of
evil fortune.

When Gualtieri had done this, he
caused it to be announced that he had
taken for wife the daughter of one of the
Counts of Panago, and causing great preparations to be made for the nuptials,
ordered Griselda to come to him, and
when she came he said—

"I am bringing this lady whom I have
recently taken, and intend to do her
honour in her first coming hither, and
thou knowest that I have not in the
palace any women who know how to set
out the rooms, or to do many other things
which are suitable for such a feast ; and

since thou knowest better than any person the things of the house, put then in order whatever has to be done, and invite what ladies thou wilt, and receive them just as if thou wert the lady of the house; then, when the nuptials have been celebrated, thou canst go back again to thine own house."

Although these words pierced like a knife to the heart of Griselda, because she could not put aside the love she bore him so easily as she had her good fortune, she replied, "My lord, I am ready and prepared." And then she went in her tattered and coarse rags into the palace, from which she had just before gone out in her smock, commenced to sweep the rooms and put them in order, caused the arras and carpets in the reception-rooms to be got ready, put the kitchen in order, and put her hands to all things, even as if

she were a little scullery - maid of the
house ; and she did not rest until she had
got everything ordered and arranged as it
should be. And immediately afterwards
she caused all the ladies of the country
to be invited on behalf of Gualtieri, and
began to get the feast ready. And when
the day of the nuptials came, she received
the ladies who came to her with all her
poor rags on her back, but with the spirit
and courtesy of a lady, and with a pleasant
countenance.

Gualtieri, who had caused his children
to be brought up carefully in Bologna,
at the house of his kinswoman who was
married to one of the Counts of Panago
(the girl being twelve years old, and the
most beautiful thing that could be seen,
and the boy six), had sent to Bologna to
his kinsman, praying that he would be
pleased to come with this his daughter

Griselda went cheerfully to meet her, saying, "Welcome, my lady!"

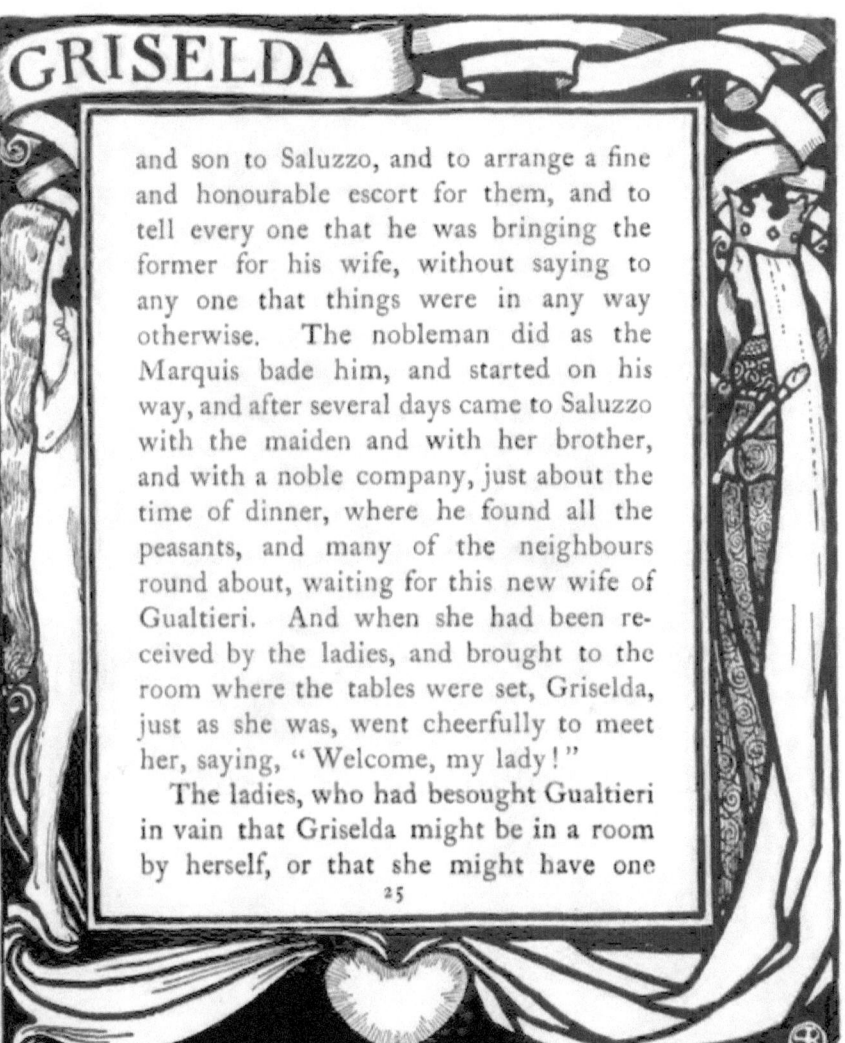

and son to Saluzzo, and to arrange a fine and honourable escort for them, and to tell every one that he was bringing the former for his wife, without saying to any one that things were in any way otherwise. The nobleman did as the Marquis bade him, and started on his way, and after several days came to Saluzzo with the maiden and with her brother, and with a noble company, just about the time of dinner, where he found all the peasants, and many of the neighbours round about, waiting for this new wife of Gualtieri. And when she had been received by the ladies, and brought to the room where the tables were set, Griselda, just as she was, went cheerfully to meet her, saying, "Welcome, my lady!"

The ladies, who had besought Gualtieri in vain that Griselda might be in a room by herself, or that she might have one

25

of the robes that she had previously had, so that she should not go thus before strangers, were set to table, and they commenced to serve. The young girl was looked upon by all, and each one said that Gualtieri had made a good exchange ; but among the rest Griselda praised her much, both her and her little brother.

Gualtieri, having at last thought that he had seen enough of his wife's patience, and seeing that in no way did change of circumstances change her, and being certain that this was not through any stupidity of mind—because he knew that she was most wise—thought it was about time to remove that bitterness which he knew she felt beneath her steadfast aspect. So he ordered her to come to him, and in presence of all men said to her with a smile, "What thinkest thou of our spouse?"

"My lord," replied Griselda, "she pleaseth me right well, and if it be that she is as wise as she is beautiful, which I fully believe, I do not doubt that you may live with her the happiest lord in the world. But I pray you with all my heart that you do not inflict upon her such pangs as you gave that other that was yours ; for I hardly think she could possibly bear it, since she is younger, and brought up in all tenderness, whereas that one was accustomed to continual hardship from a little girl."

Gualtieri, seeing that though she firmly believed that this one was to be his wife, she did not speak to him less than well, caused her to be set at his side, and said to her—

"Griselda, it is now time for thee to reap the fruit of thy long patience, and for those who have thought me cruel and

unjust, and a beast, to know that what I
have done has been done with this end in
view, that thou mightest learn to be a
wife, and that they might know how to
choose and keep one, while I should gain
for myself perpetual peace while I have
to live with thee, which when I came to
take a wife I had great fear I should never
possess.   Wherefore, in order to prove
thee, I have tried and entreated thee
harshly in all ways, and now, since I am
assured that neither in word nor in deed
hast thou in any way departed from my
pleasure, and it appears to me that I have
from thee that very happiness which I
desire, I intend to render to thee in one
hour all that I have taken away from
thee in many days, and to soothe with
the greatest sweetness the pangs which I
caused thee.   Therefore with joyful mind
know that this girl whom thou didst take

The ladies took off her rags and clothed her in a noble robe

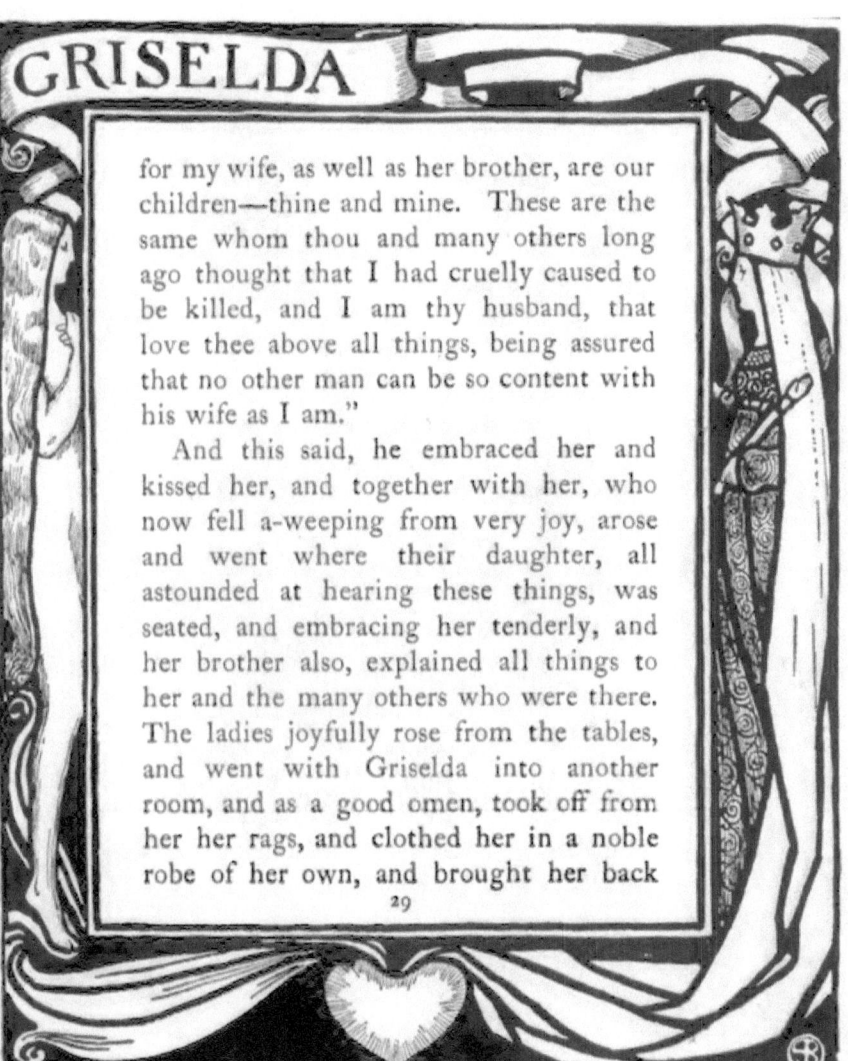

for my wife, as well as her brother, are our children—thine and mine. These are the same whom thou and many others long ago thought that I had cruelly caused to be killed, and I am thy husband, that love thee above all things, being assured that no other man can be so content with his wife as I am."

And this said, he embraced her and kissed her, and together with her, who now fell a-weeping from very joy, arose and went where their daughter, all astounded at hearing these things, was seated, and embracing her tenderly, and her brother also, explained all things to her and the many others who were there. The ladies joyfully rose from the tables, and went with Griselda into another room, and as a good omen, took off from her her rags, and clothed her in a noble robe of her own, and brought her back

29

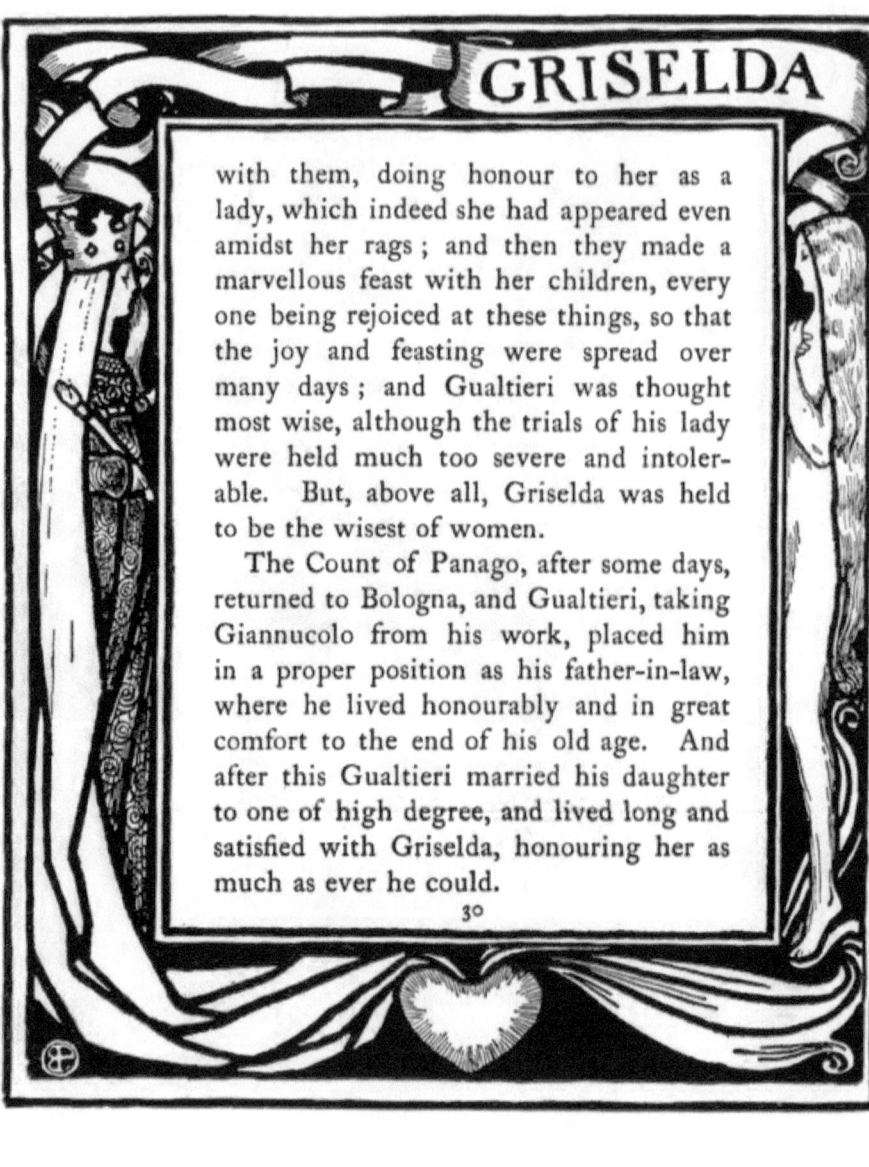

with them, doing honour to her as a lady, which indeed she had appeared even amidst her rags ; and then they made a marvellous feast with her children, every one being rejoiced at these things, so that the joy and feasting were spread over many days ; and Gualtieri was thought most wise, although the trials of his lady were held much too severe and intolerable. But, above all, Griselda was held to be the wisest of women.

The Count of Panago, after some days, returned to Bologna, and Gualtieri, taking Giannucolo from his work, placed him in a proper position as his father-in-law, where he lived honourably and in great comfort to the end of his old age. And after this Gualtieri married his daughter to one of high degree, and lived long and satisfied with Griselda, honouring her as much as ever he could.

30

Here endeth

the Tale of

Griselda

Here beginneth
the Tale of
Saladin and Torello

XIX

SALADIN & TORELLO

SOME say that at the time of the Emperor Frederick the First, a general Crusade was undertaken by the Christians to regain the Holy Land. Now Saladin, a most valiant lord, and at that time Soldan of Babylon, heard of this a great time before, and proposed to himself to see in person the preparations of the Christian lords for that Crusade, so that he might the better provide against it. Having set all things aright in Egypt, he made semblance of going upon a pilgrimage, and set out in guise of a merchant with two of his most important and discreetest men, and with three attendants. After having passed through many Christian provinces, it chanced that as they were riding through Lombardy to cross over to the other side of the mountains, they came from Milan towards Pavia about vesper time, and

35

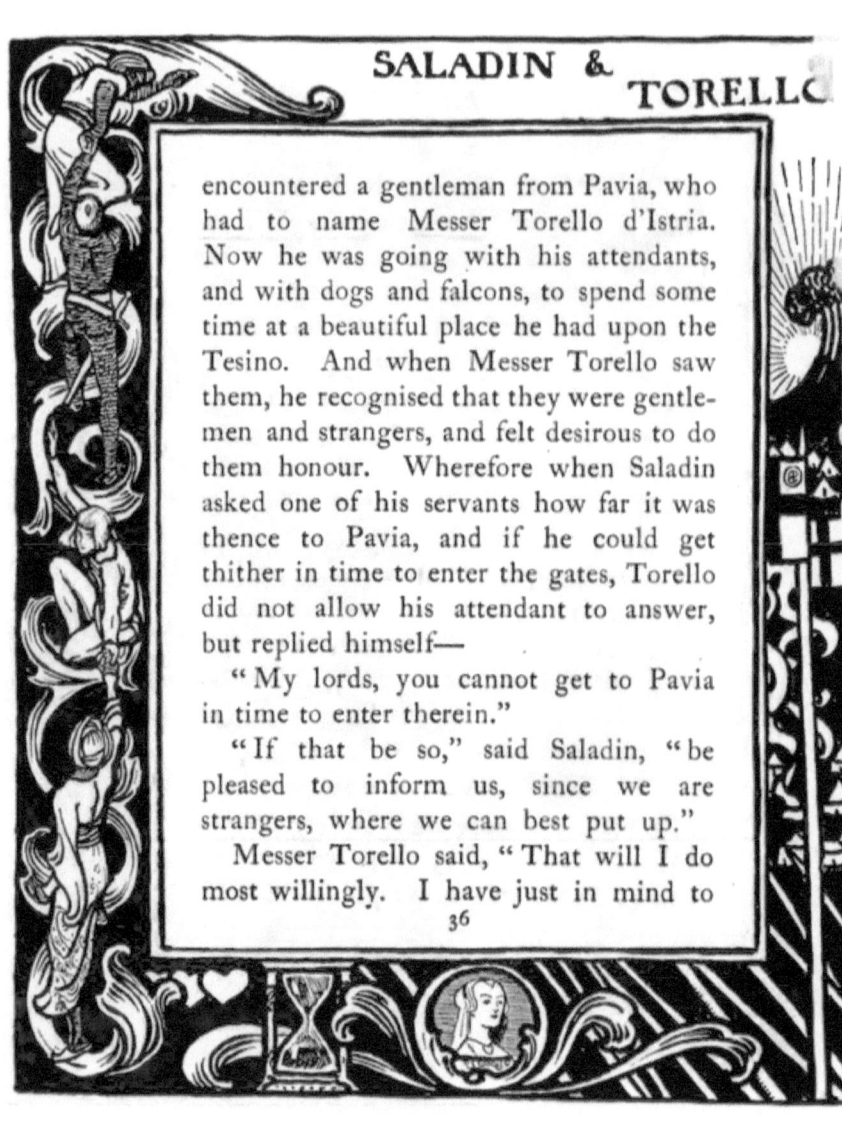

encountered a gentleman from Pavia, who had to name Messer Torello d'Istria. Now he was going with his attendants, and with dogs and falcons, to spend some time at a beautiful place he had upon the Tesino. And when Messer Torello saw them, he recognised that they were gentlemen and strangers, and felt desirous to do them honour. Wherefore when Saladin asked one of his servants how far it was thence to Pavia, and if he could get thither in time to enter the gates, Torello did not allow his attendant to answer, but replied himself—

"My lords, you cannot get to Pavia in time to enter therein."

"If that be so," said Saladin, "be pleased to inform us, since we are strangers, where we can best put up."

Messer Torello said, "That will I do most willingly. I have just in mind to

36

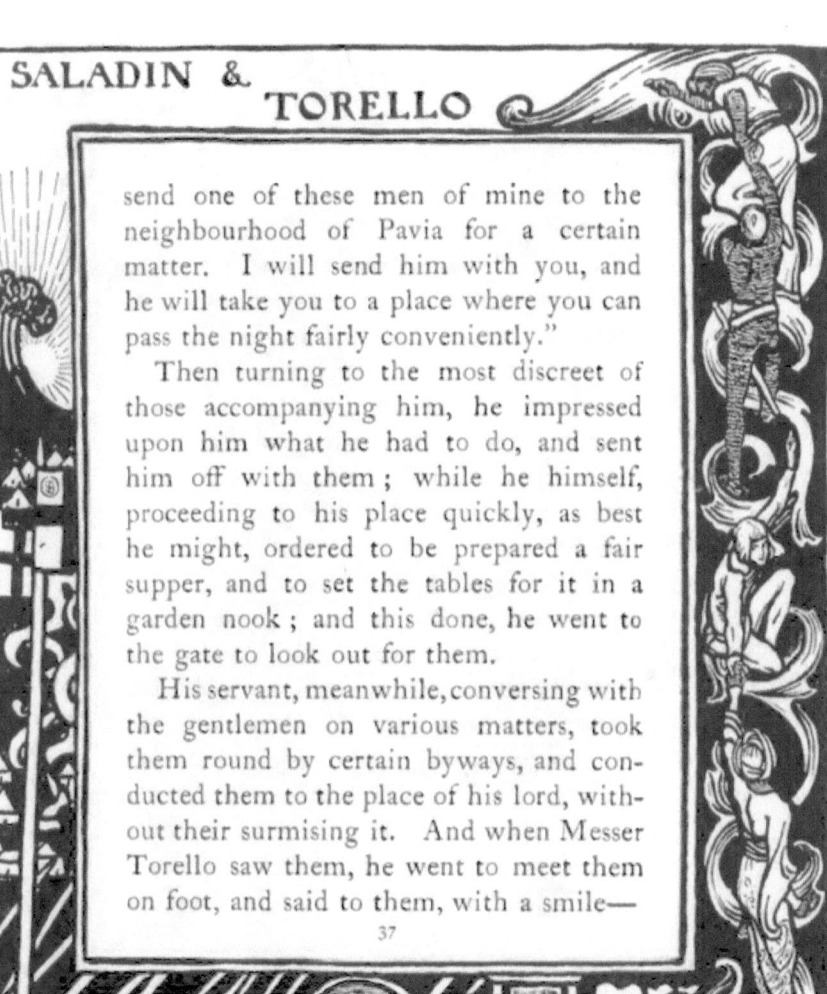

send one of these men of mine to the neighbourhood of Pavia for a certain matter. I will send him with you, and he will take you to a place where you can pass the night fairly conveniently."

Then turning to the most discreet of those accompanying him, he impressed upon him what he had to do, and sent him off with them; while he himself, proceeding to his place quickly, as best he might, ordered to be prepared a fair supper, and to set the tables for it in a garden nook; and this done, he went to the gate to look out for them.

His servant, meanwhile, conversing with the gentlemen on various matters, took them round by certain byways, and conducted them to the place of his lord, without their surmising it. And when Messer Torello saw them, he went to meet them on foot, and said to them, with a smile—

37

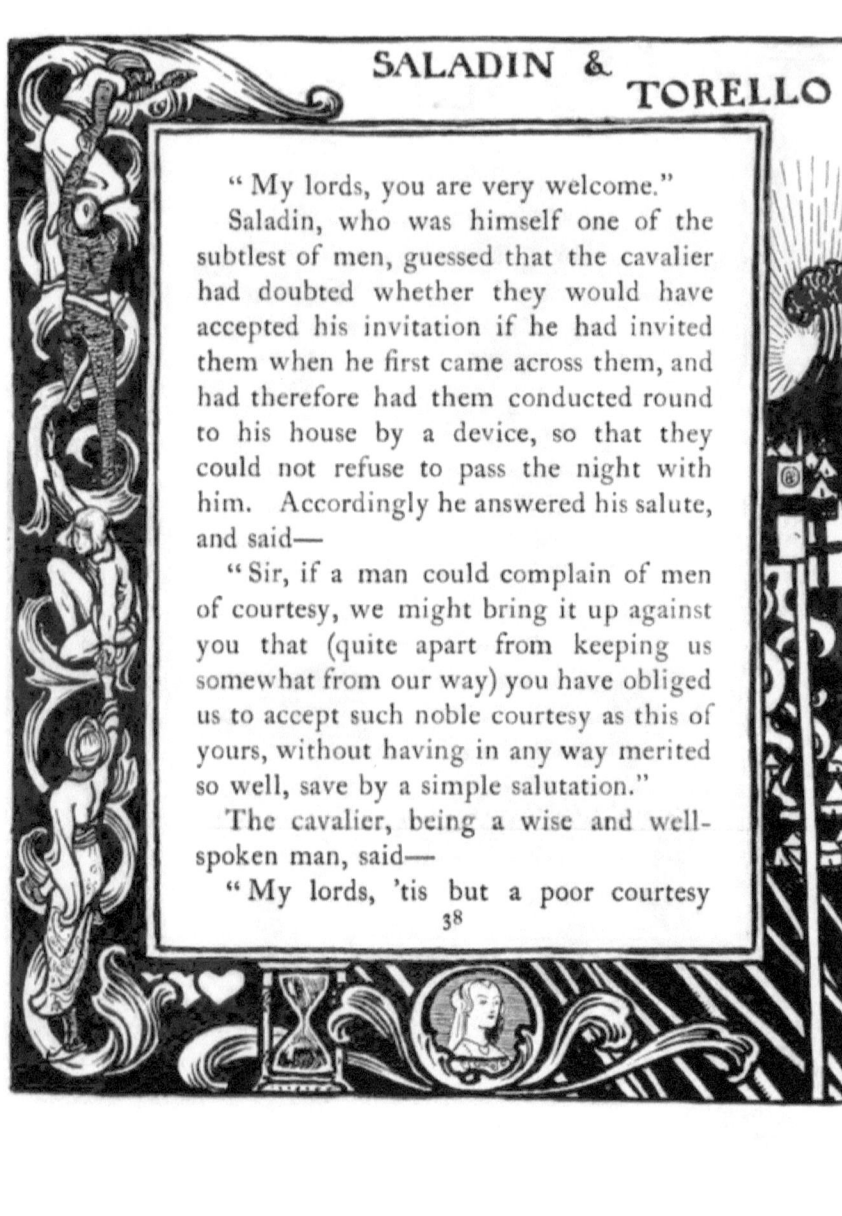

"My lords, you are very welcome."

Saladin, who was himself one of the subtlest of men, guessed that the cavalier had doubted whether they would have accepted his invitation if he had invited them when he first came across them, and had therefore had them conducted round to his house by a device, so that they could not refuse to pass the night with him. Accordingly he answered his salute, and said—

"Sir, if a man could complain of men of courtesy, we might bring it up against you that (quite apart from keeping us somewhat from our way) you have obliged us to accept such noble courtesy as this of yours, without having in any way merited so well, save by a simple salutation."

The cavalier, being a wise and well-spoken man, said—

"My lords, 'tis but a poor courtesy

38

that you are receiving from me, compared with that which befits you, so far as I can judge by your appearance, but in very deed, outside Pavia you could have been received in no place that was worthy ; wherefore take it not ill that you have gone a little out of your way, in order to have a little less discomfort." And as he thus spoke, his people came around them, and, when they were dismounted, took charge of their horses.

Messer Torello led the three gentlemen to the chambers prepared for them, where he caused them to be relieved of their boots, and to be refreshed somewhat with wine most cool and delectable. He kept them engaged in gentle conversation until time was for taking supper. Saladin and his companions and attendants all knew Latin, so that they both understood and were understood right well ; and this

39

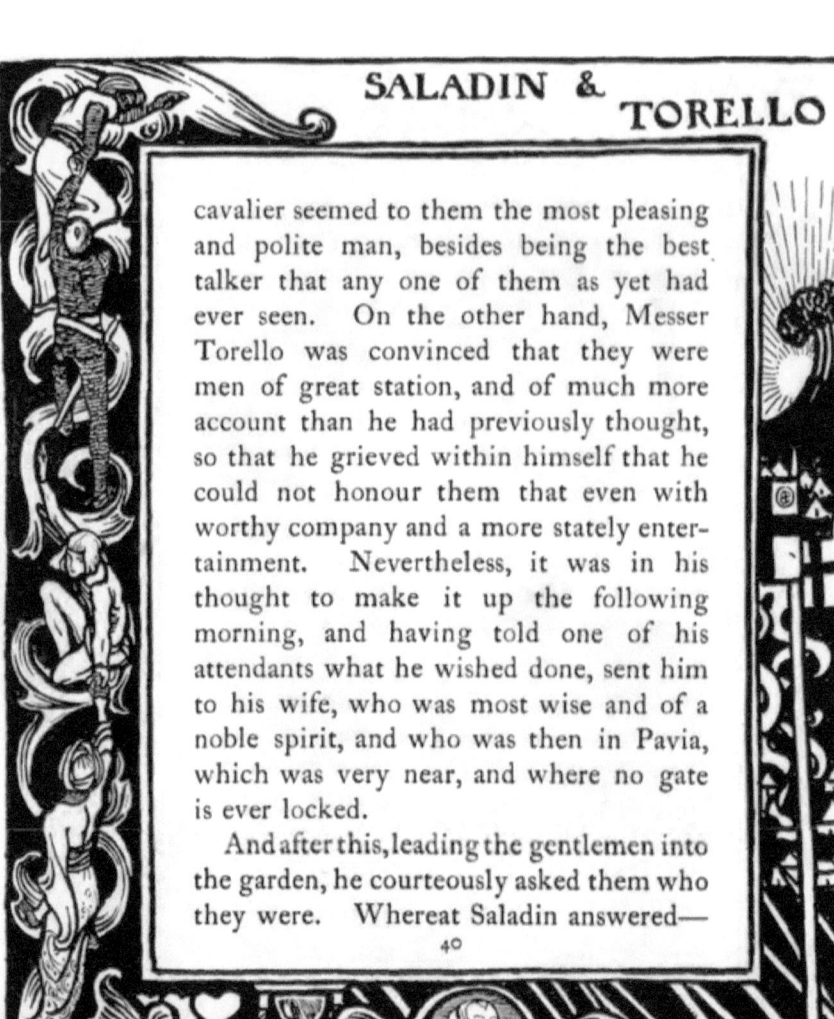

cavalier seemed to them the most pleasing and polite man, besides being the best talker that any one of them as yet had ever seen. On the other hand, Messer Torello was convinced that they were men of great station, and of much more account than he had previously thought, so that he grieved within himself that he could not honour them that even with worthy company and a more stately entertainment. Nevertheless, it was in his thought to make it up the following morning, and having told one of his attendants what he wished done, sent him to his wife, who was most wise and of a noble spirit, and who was then in Pavia, which was very near, and where no gate is ever locked.

And after this, leading the gentlemen into the garden, he courteously asked them who they were. Whereat Saladin answered—

" We are merchants of Cyprus, and we come therefrom, and go to Paris for our needs."

Then said Messer Torello, " Please God that our country may produce such gentlemen as I see Cyprus produces merchants."

And after such talk on other subjects for a while, the time came for supper, whereupon he entreated them to do the honours in placing themselves at table in due rank; and then they were served with a supper sufficiently goodly and in due order, considering that it was but improvised. Not long after the tables had been removed, Messer Torello, perceiving that they were weary, put them to repose in most stately beds, and himself in like manner, a little after, went to sleep.

The servant who had been sent to Pavia did his errand with the lady, who had a spirit not like that of a woman, but of a king, and she, in no housewifely spirit, but on a princely scale, ordered to be summoned a goodly number of the friends and household of Messer Torello, and got ready a banquet with everything most fit and on a grand scale. Also she caused to be invited to the banquet, by light of torch, many of the most noble citizens, and brought out cloths and silks and furs, and put completely in due order all that her husband had sent for her to do.

At daybreak the gentlemen arose. Messer Torello mounted his horse and went with them, and having caused his falcons to be brought to him, he led them to a neighbouring ford, where he showed them how the flight took place. But when Saladin asked for some one to conduct them to Pavia, and the best inn there, Messer Torello said—

42

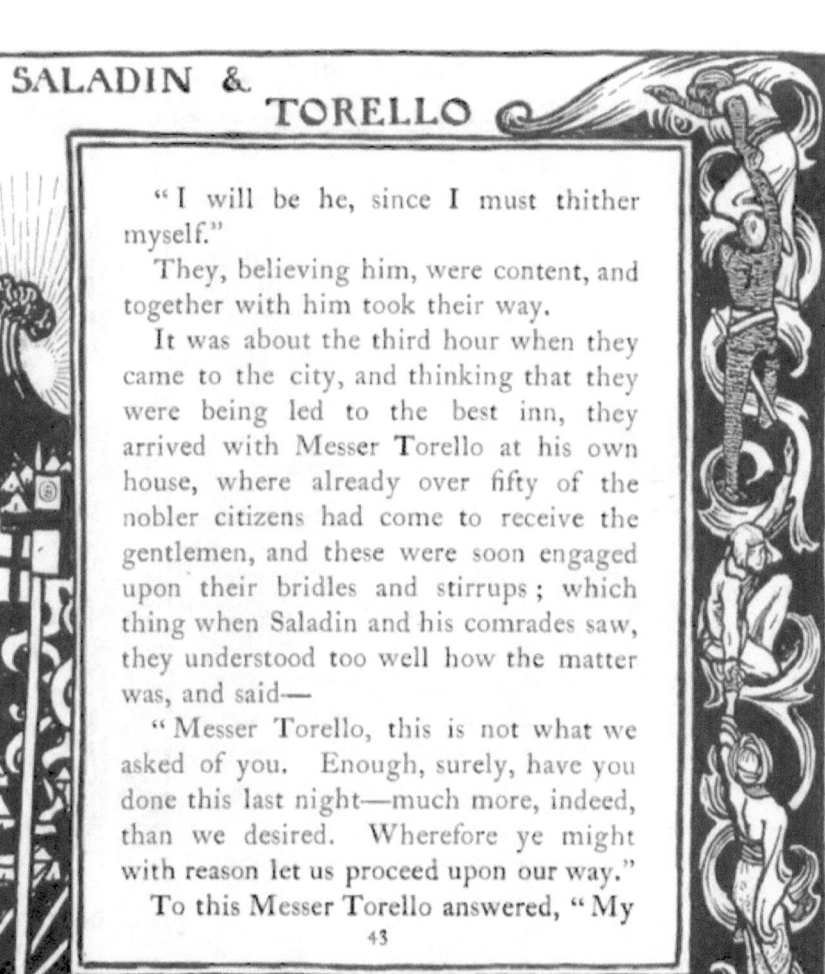

"I will be he, since I must thither myself."

They, believing him, were content, and together with him took their way.

It was about the third hour when they came to the city, and thinking that they were being led to the best inn, they arrived with Messer Torello at his own house, where already over fifty of the nobler citizens had come to receive the gentlemen, and these were soon engaged upon their bridles and stirrups; which thing when Saladin and his comrades saw, they understood too well how the matter was, and said—

"Messer Torello, this is not what we asked of you. Enough, surely, have you done this last night—much more, indeed, than we desired. Wherefore ye might with reason let us proceed upon our way."

To this Messer Torello answered, "My

43

lords, for that which was done yestreen
I was more indebted to fortune than to
you, in that I found you on the road at
an hour when you must needs come to my
poor house, but for that which may take
place now, this morning, I shall be be-
holden to you, and together with me, all
these gentlemen who are about you ; but
if you think you can with courtesy refuse
to dine with them, ye may do so an you
will."

Saladin and his friends, being conquered
by this, dismounted, and being received
joyously by the gentlemen, were led to
their rooms, which had been most richly
apparelled for them, and having put off
their riding apparel and refreshed themselves somewhat, they came to the saloon,
which had been splendidly prepared.
Water having been poured upon their
hands, and having been put at table in

the most stately order and seemliest, they were served with much magnificence from many meats, so much so, that if the Emperor himself had come there, they could not have done him more of honour ; and although Saladin and his company were great lords, and used to seeing things on a great scale, nevertheless they marvelled much at this, and it appeared to them all the greater, having respect to the quality of the cavalier, whom they knew was a mere citizen and no lord.

The eating finished, and the tables removed, after they had talked of other things awhile, the heat being great, the gentlemen of Pavia all went to take their repose at Messer Torello's desire. He himself, being left alone with those three, entered into a room with them, and so that there might remain nothing dear to him which they had not seen, caused his worthy wife to be summoned. And she came before them and pleasantly saluted them, being most beauteous and tall in person, arrayed in rich vestments, and having on either side her two little boys, who seemed like two angels. And they, seeing her, rose to their feet and received her with due deference, and caused her to sit among them, and made merry with her two fine boys. Now, while she was engaged in pleasant conversation with them, Torello departed for a short time, and she in courteous wise asked whence they came and whither they were going, and to this the gentlemen made the same reply as they had given to Messer Torello. Then the lady said with joyful visage—

"Then I see that my woman's wit will be of use. Wherefore I pray you to do me a special grace, not to refuse nor

46

BYAM·SHAW

Vaus & Crampton, Sc.

He caused his worthy wife to be summoned

reckon lightly this little gift which I am about to have sent for; but if you bethink you that women, with their little heart, can give but little things, pray take it, having regard to the goodwill of her that gives, rather than to the greatness of the gift."

Thereupon she caused to be brought for each of them two robes, one lined with silk, and the other with miniver, by no means the garb of citizens or of merchants, but of lords, and besides these, three doublets of taffety and linen therewith. And she said—

"Take these. I have clothed my own lord in robes like yours. As for the other things, considering that you are far away from your ladies, and the length of road you have passed through, and that which is still to come, and that merchants are somewhat delicate and nice, you may

47

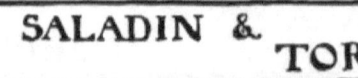
possibly care for them, though they be of little worth."

The stranger gentlemen marvelled much, and clearly saw that Messer Torello wished to leave undone no part of courtesy towards them ; and when they saw the splendour of the robes (far above the quality of merchants), they were even in doubt whether they had been recognised of him. But one of them merely replied to the lady—

"These, madam, are very fine things, and not so easily to be accepted, but that your prayers force us thereto, seeing that it is impossible to say 'No' to them."

This done, and Messer Torello having already come back, the lady, commending them to God, took her leave of them, and caused their attendants to be provided with similar things, suitable for their condition. Messer Torello, with many

48

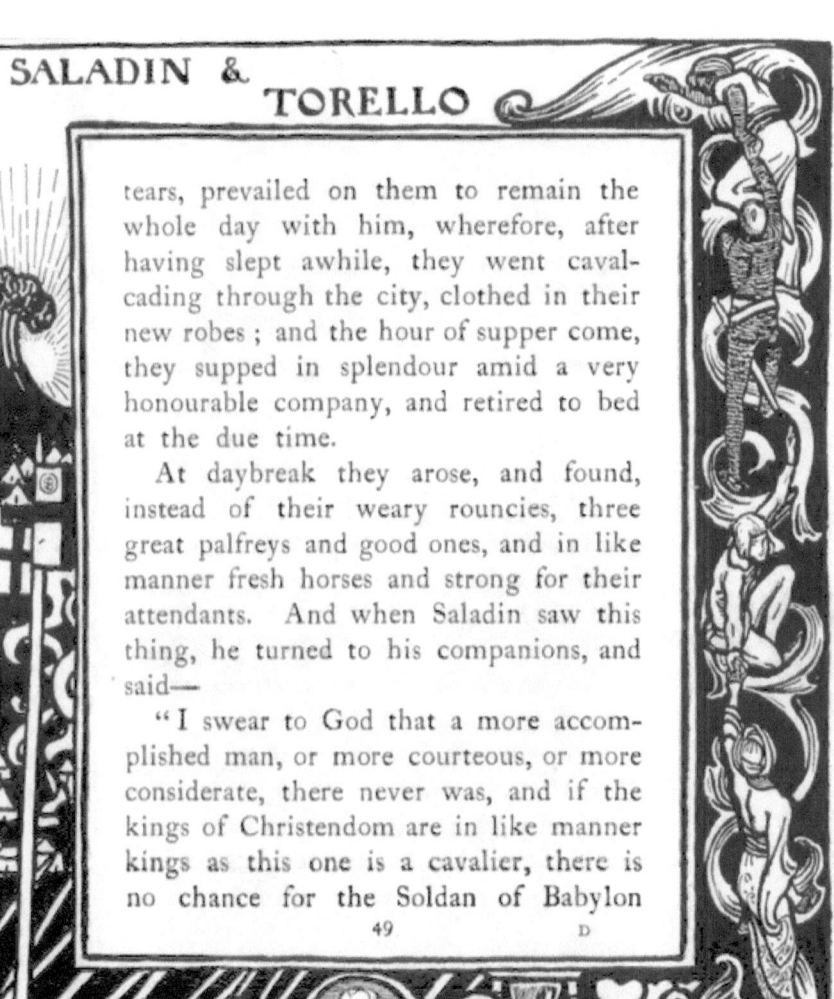

tears, prevailed on them to remain the whole day with him, wherefore, after having slept awhile, they went caval-cading through the city, clothed in their new robes ; and the hour of supper come, they supped in splendour amid a very honourable company, and retired to bed at the due time.

At daybreak they arose, and found, instead of their weary rouncies, three great palfreys and good ones, and in like manner fresh horses and strong for their attendants. And when Saladin saw this thing, he turned to his companions, and said—

"I swear to God that a more accom-plished man, or more courteous, or more considerate, there never was, and if the kings of Christendom are in like manner kings as this one is a cavalier, there is no chance for the Soldan of Babylon

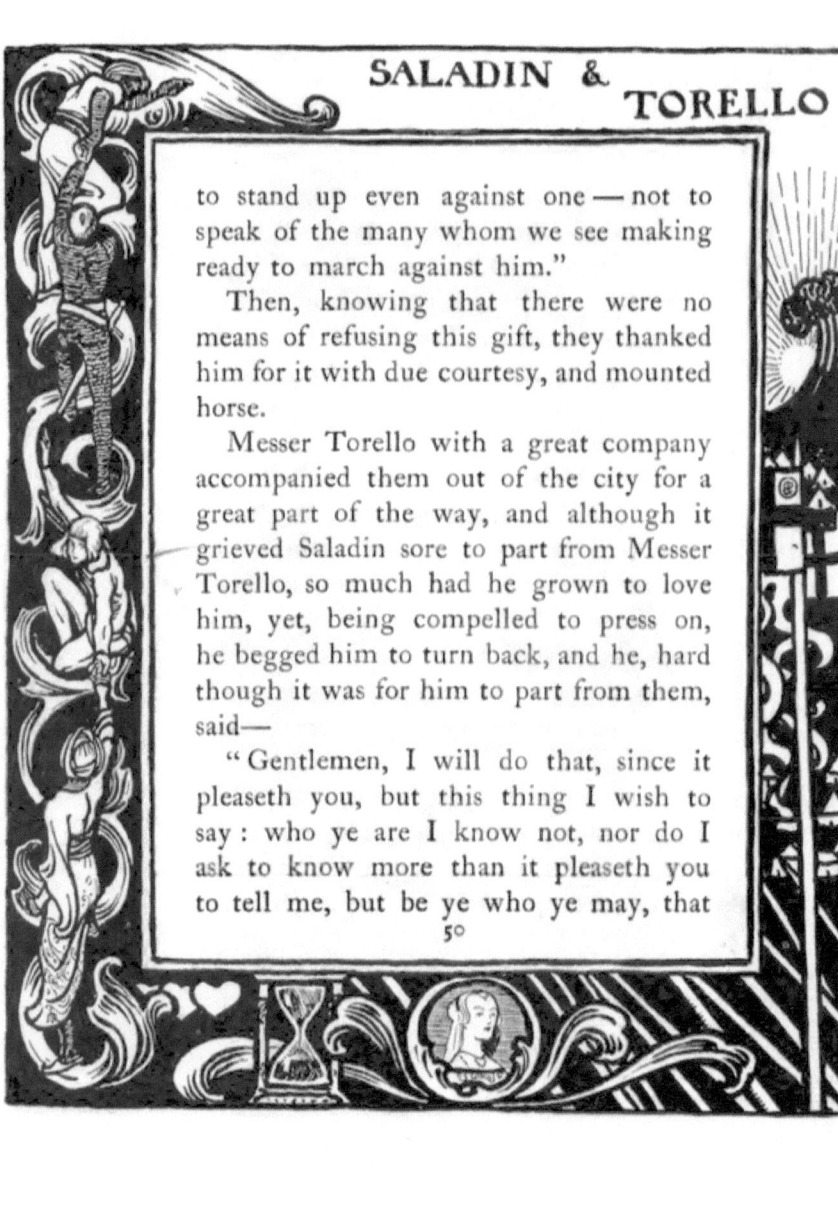

to stand up even against one — not to speak of the many whom we see making ready to march against him."

Then, knowing that there were no means of refusing this gift, they thanked him for it with due courtesy, and mounted horse.

Messer Torello with a great company accompanied them out of the city for a great part of the way, and although it grieved Saladin sore to part from Messer Torello, so much had he grown to love him, yet, being compelled to press on, he begged him to turn back, and he, hard though it was for him to part from them, said—

"Gentlemen, I will do that, since it pleaseth you, but this thing I wish to say : who ye are I know not, nor do I ask to know more than it pleaseth you to tell me, but be ye who ye may, that

ye are merchants ye cannot cause me to believe, at this or any other time, and so to God I commend you."

Saladin, after having taken leave of all Messer Torello's companions, answered him, and said—

"Sir, it may possibly perchance that we may cause you to see some of our merchandise, by which we may confirm your belief, but now God be with you."

Thus Saladin, with his companions, parted from them with the fullest intention that if life lasted, and if the war which he expected did not prevent him, to do at some time no less honour to Messer Torello than he had done unto him ; and often he would speak to his companions of him, and of his lady, and of all their things and acts and deeds, much commending everything.

But after he had encircled, not without

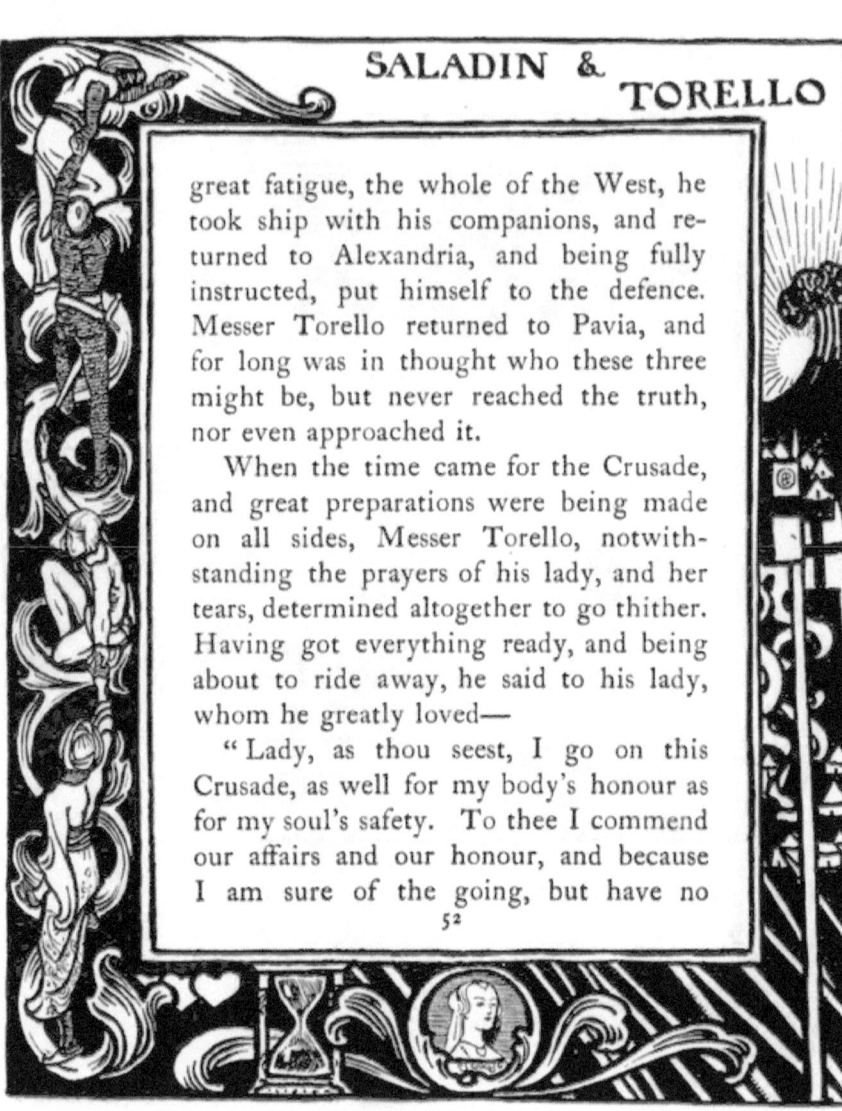

great fatigue, the whole of the West, he
took ship with his companions, and returned to Alexandria, and being fully
instructed, put himself to the defence.
Messer Torello returned to Pavia, and
for long was in thought who these three
might be, but never reached the truth,
nor even approached it.

When the time came for the Crusade,
and great preparations were being made
on all sides, Messer Torello, notwithstanding the prayers of his lady, and her
tears, determined altogether to go thither.
Having got everything ready, and being
about to ride away, he said to his lady,
whom he greatly loved—

"Lady, as thou seest, I go on this
Crusade, as well for my body's honour as
for my soul's safety. To thee I commend
our affairs and our honour, and because
I am sure of the going, but have no

52

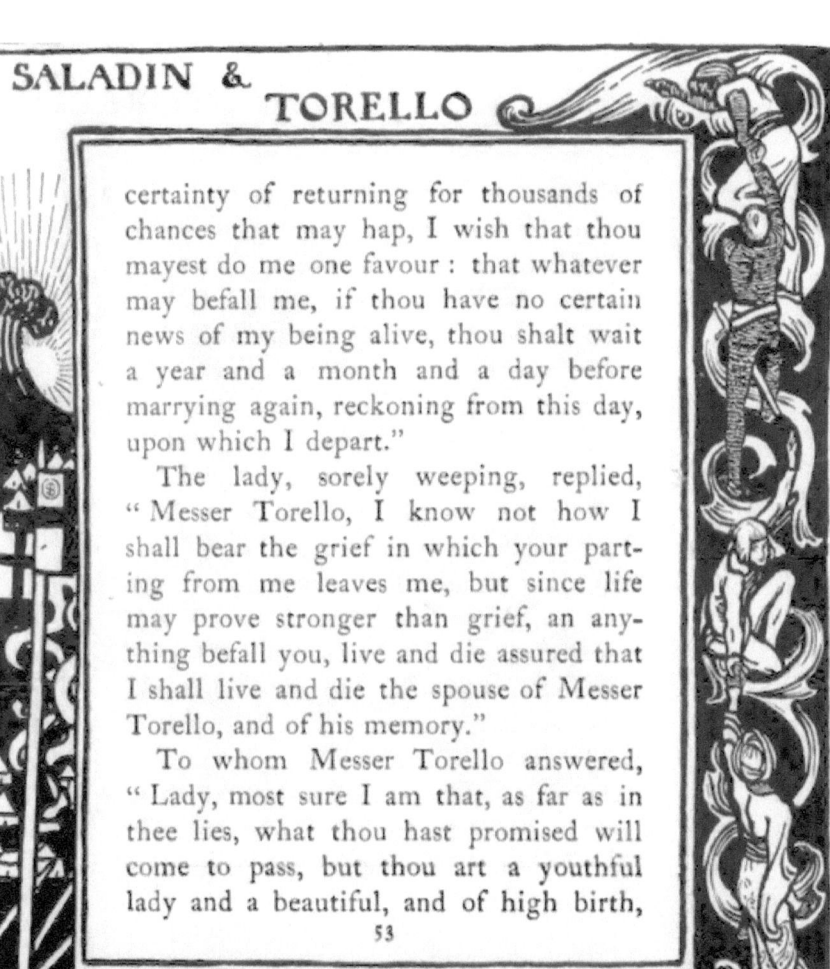

certainty of returning for thousands of chances that may hap, I wish that thou mayest do me one favour : that whatever may befall me, if thou have no certain news of my being alive, thou shalt wait a year and a month and a day before marrying again, reckoning from this day, upon which I depart."

The lady, sorely weeping, replied, "Messer Torello, I know not how I shall bear the grief in which your parting from me leaves me, but since life may prove stronger than grief, an anything befall you, live and die assured that I shall live and die the spouse of Messer Torello, and of his memory."

To whom Messer Torello answered, "Lady, most sure I am that, as far as in thee lies, what thou hast promised will come to pass, but thou art a youthful lady and a beautiful, and of high birth,

53

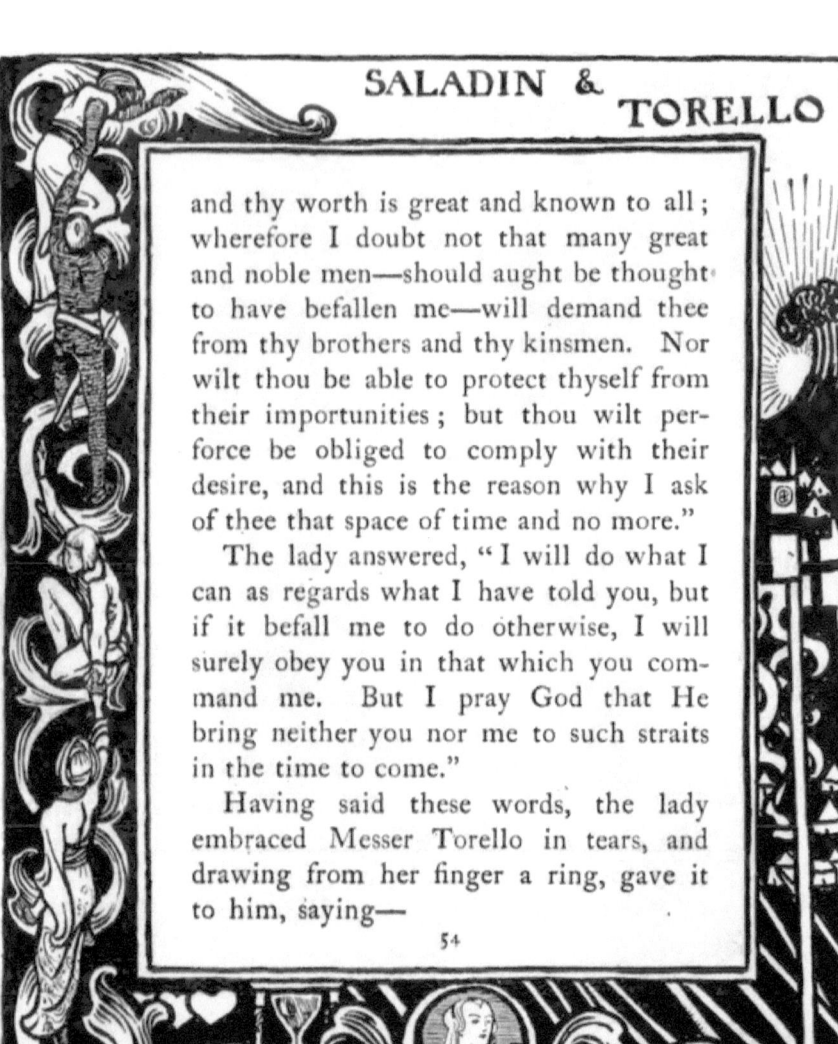

and thy worth is great and known to all; wherefore I doubt not that many great and noble men—should aught be thought to have befallen me—will demand thee from thy brothers and thy kinsmen. Nor wilt thou be able to protect thyself from their importunities; but thou wilt perforce be obliged to comply with their desire, and this is the reason why I ask of thee that space of time and no more."

The lady answered, "I will do what I can as regards what I have told you, but if it befall me to do otherwise, I will surely obey you in that which you command me. But I pray God that He bring neither you nor me to such straits in the time to come."

Having said these words, the lady embraced Messer Torello in tears, and drawing from her finger a ring, gave it to him, saying—

54

Torello, saying adieu to everyone, started on his journey

"If it chance that I die before that I see you again, remember me whensoe'er you look upon it."

Torello, taking it, mounted his horse, and saying adieu to every one, started on his journey, and arriving at Genoa with his company, embarked at once on a galley, and in a short time arrived at Acre, where he joined the rest of the army of the Christians. Almost at once there broke out a most severe pestilence and mortality. During this, whether it be through the skill or the good fortune of Saladin, almost all the rest of the Christians who had escaped from it were captured without risk, and were divided and imprisoned in many cities. Among those who were taken was Messer Torello, and he was placed in prison at Alexandria. There, being unknown, and fearing to make himself known, he was constrained

by his need to take to the training of
hawks, of which he was a great master.
By this means he came to the notice of
Saladin, wherefore he took him from
prison, and retained him as his falconer.
Messer Torello, not being called by any
other name than "the Christian" (for he
did not recognise the Soldan, nor the
Soldan him), kept his thoughts fixed
upon Pavia, and made many attempts to
flee, but they were of none avail.

Now, certain Genoese having come as
ambassadors to Saladin to ransom certain
of their fellow-citizens, and being about
to depart, he thought to write to his lady,
how that he was alive, and would return
to her as soon as possible, and that she
should await him. Having done this,
he sorely begged one of the ambassadors,
whom he knew, to arrange that this
should come to the hand of the Abbot

56

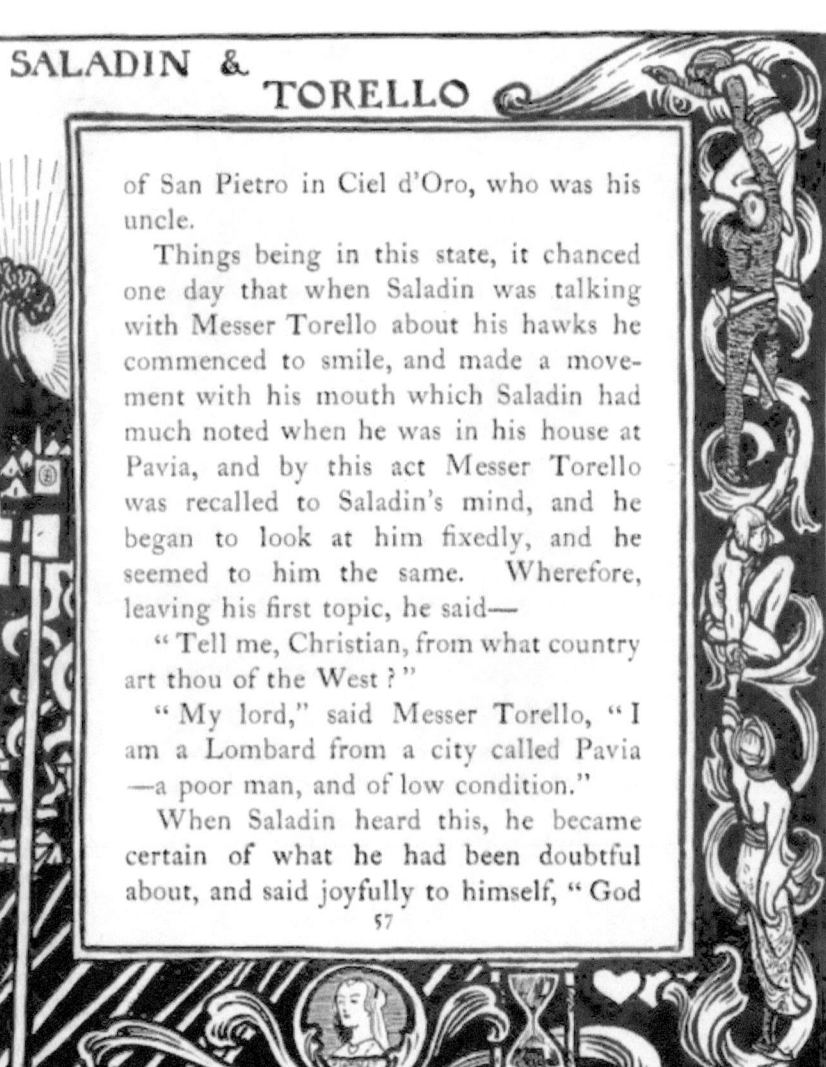

of San Pietro in Ciel d'Oro, who was his uncle.

Things being in this state, it chanced one day that when Saladin was talking with Messer Torello about his hawks he commenced to smile, and made a movement with his mouth which Saladin had much noted when he was in his house at Pavia, and by this act Messer Torello was recalled to Saladin's mind, and he began to look at him fixedly, and he seemed to him the same. Wherefore, leaving his first topic, he said—

"Tell me, Christian, from what country art thou of the West?"

"My lord," said Messer Torello, "I am a Lombard from a city called Pavia—a poor man, and of low condition."

When Saladin heard this, he became certain of what he had been doubtful about, and said joyfully to himself, "God

57

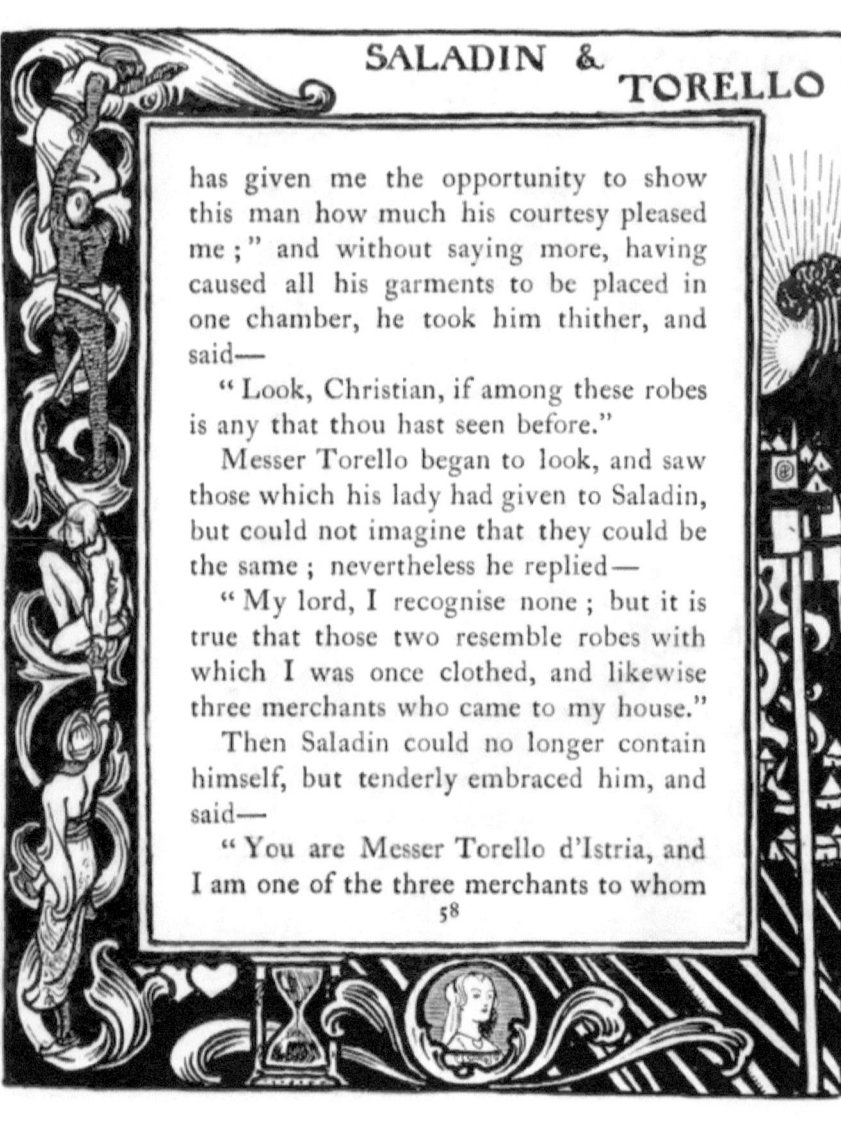

has given me the opportunity to show this man how much his courtesy pleased me ; " and without saying more, having caused all his garments to be placed in one chamber, he took him thither, and said—

"Look, Christian, if among these robes is any that thou hast seen before."

Messer Torello began to look, and saw those which his lady had given to Saladin, but could not imagine that they could be the same ; nevertheless he replied—

"My lord, I recognise none ; but it is true that those two resemble robes with which I was once clothed, and likewise three merchants who came to my house."

Then Saladin could no longer contain himself, but tenderly embraced him, and said—

"You are Messer Torello d'Istria, and I am one of the three merchants to whom

58

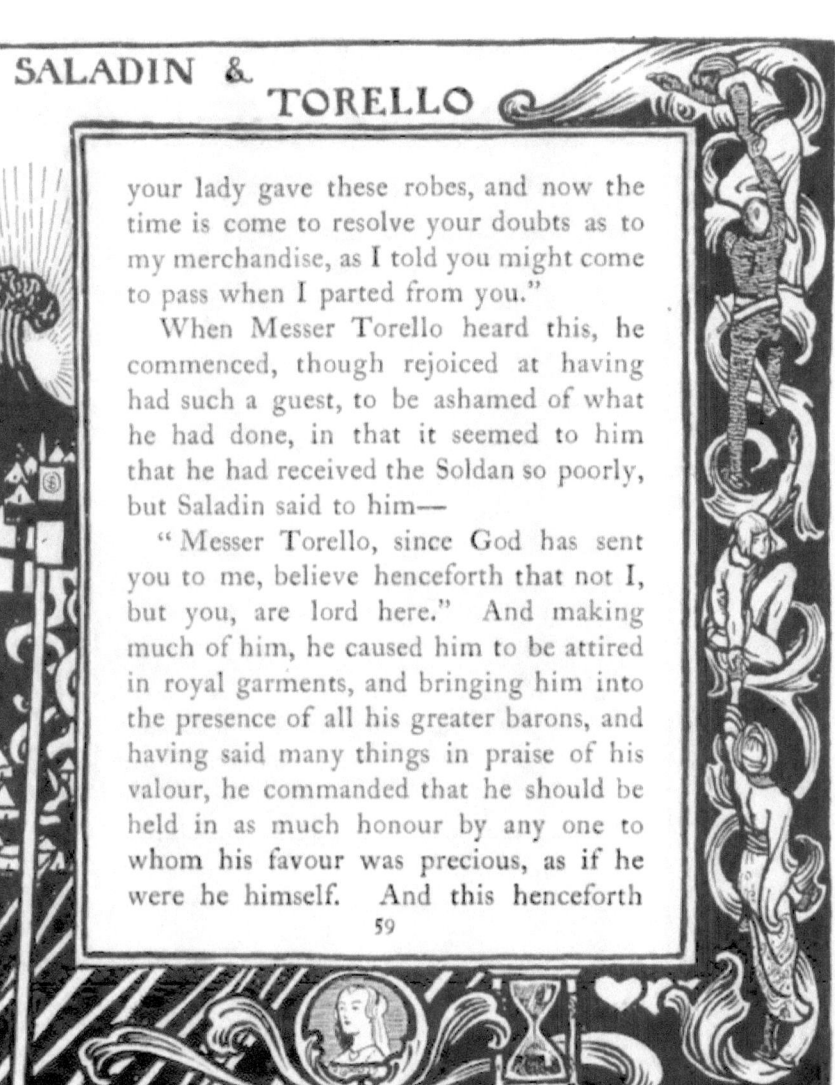

your lady gave these robes, and now the time is come to resolve your doubts as to my merchandise, as I told you might come to pass when I parted from you."

When Messer Torello heard this, he commenced, though rejoiced at having had such a guest, to be ashamed of what he had done, in that it seemed to him that he had received the Soldan so poorly, but Saladin said to him—

"Messer Torello, since God has sent you to me, believe henceforth that not I, but you, are lord here." And making much of him, he caused him to be attired in royal garments, and bringing him into the presence of all his greater barons, and having said many things in praise of his valour, he commanded that he should be held in as much honour by any one to whom his favour was precious, as if he were he himself. And this henceforth

59

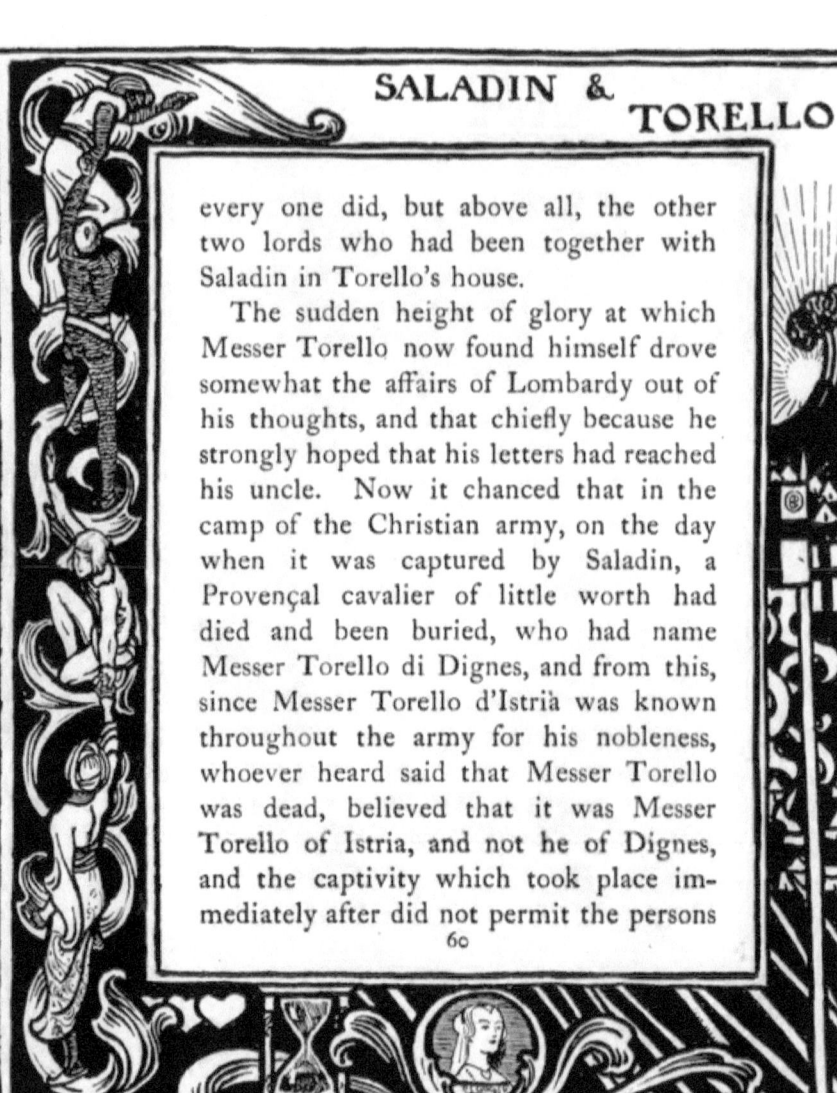

every one did, but above all, the other two lords who had been together with Saladin in Torello's house.

The sudden height of glory at which Messer Torello now found himself drove somewhat the affairs of Lombardy out of his thoughts, and that chiefly because he strongly hoped that his letters had reached his uncle. Now it chanced that in the camp of the Christian army, on the day when it was captured by Saladin, a Provençal cavalier of little worth had died and been buried, who had name Messer Torello di Dignes, and from this, since Messer Torello d'Istrià was known throughout the army for his nobleness, whoever heard said that Messer Torello was dead, believed that it was Messer Torello of Istria, and not he of Dignes, and the captivity which took place immediately after did not permit the persons

60

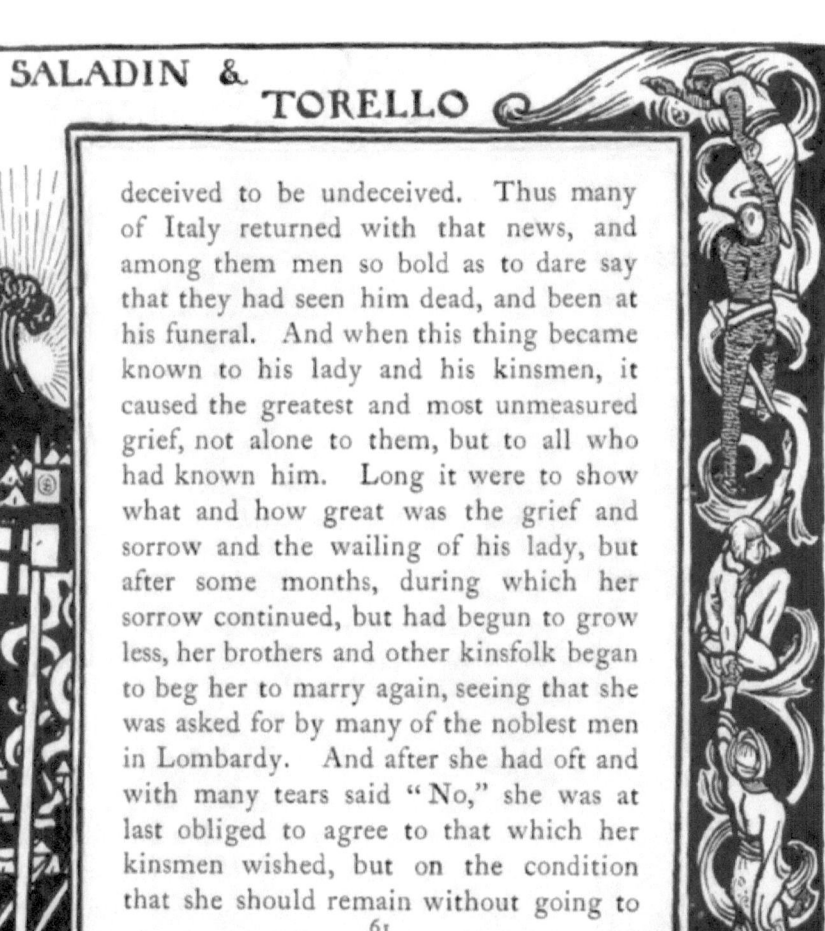

deceived to be undeceived. Thus many
of Italy returned with that news, and
among them men so bold as to dare say
that they had seen him dead, and been at
his funeral. And when this thing became
known to his lady and his kinsmen, it
caused the greatest and most unmeasured
grief, not alone to them, but to all who
had known him. Long it were to show
what and how great was the grief and
sorrow and the wailing of his lady, but
after some months, during which her
sorrow continued, but had begun to grow
less, her brothers and other kinsfolk began
to beg her to marry again, seeing that she
was asked for by many of the noblest men
in Lombardy. And after she had oft and
with many tears said "No," she was at
last obliged to agree to that which her
kinsmen wished, but on the condition
that she should remain without going to

61

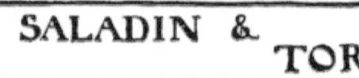

a husband as long as she had promised Messer Torello.

While in Pavia the affairs of this lady were at such a pass that the last week of the time when she would have to go to her new husband was near, it chanced that Messer Torello in Alexandria saw one day one of the men whom he had seen go aboard the galley with the Genoese ambassador, when it was going to Genoa; and causing him to be summoned to him, he asked how the voyage had turned out, and when they had arrived at Genoa. But the other said—

"My lord, it was an ill voyage the galley made, as I heard in Crete, where I remained, for when it was near Sicily there arose a dangerous wind from the north, which drove her on to the sands of Barbary. Not a single one escaped,

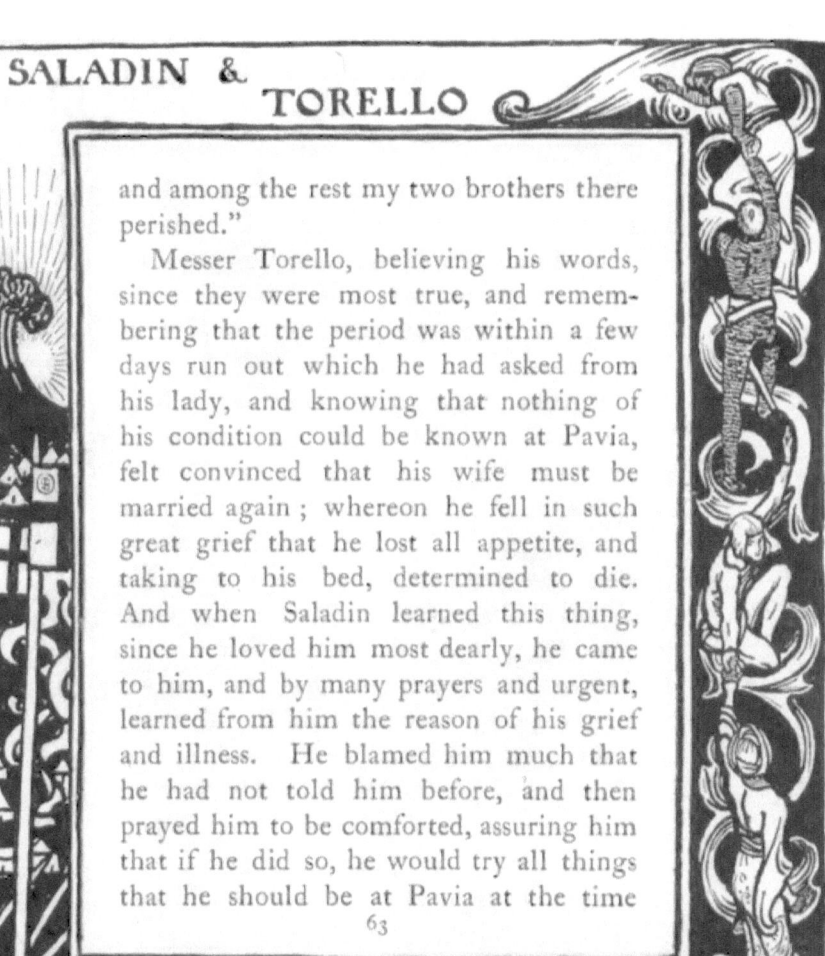

and among the rest my two brothers there
perished."

Messer Torello, believing his words,
since they were most true, and remembering that the period was within a few
days run out which he had asked from
his lady, and knowing that nothing of
his condition could be known at Pavia,
felt convinced that his wife must be
married again ; whereon he fell in such
great grief that he lost all appetite, and
taking to his bed, determined to die.
And when Saladin learned this thing,
since he loved him most dearly, he came
to him, and by many prayers and urgent,
learned from him the reason of his grief
and illness. He blamed him much that
he had not told him before, and then
prayed him to be comforted, assuring him
that if he did so, he would try all things
that he should be at Pavia at the time

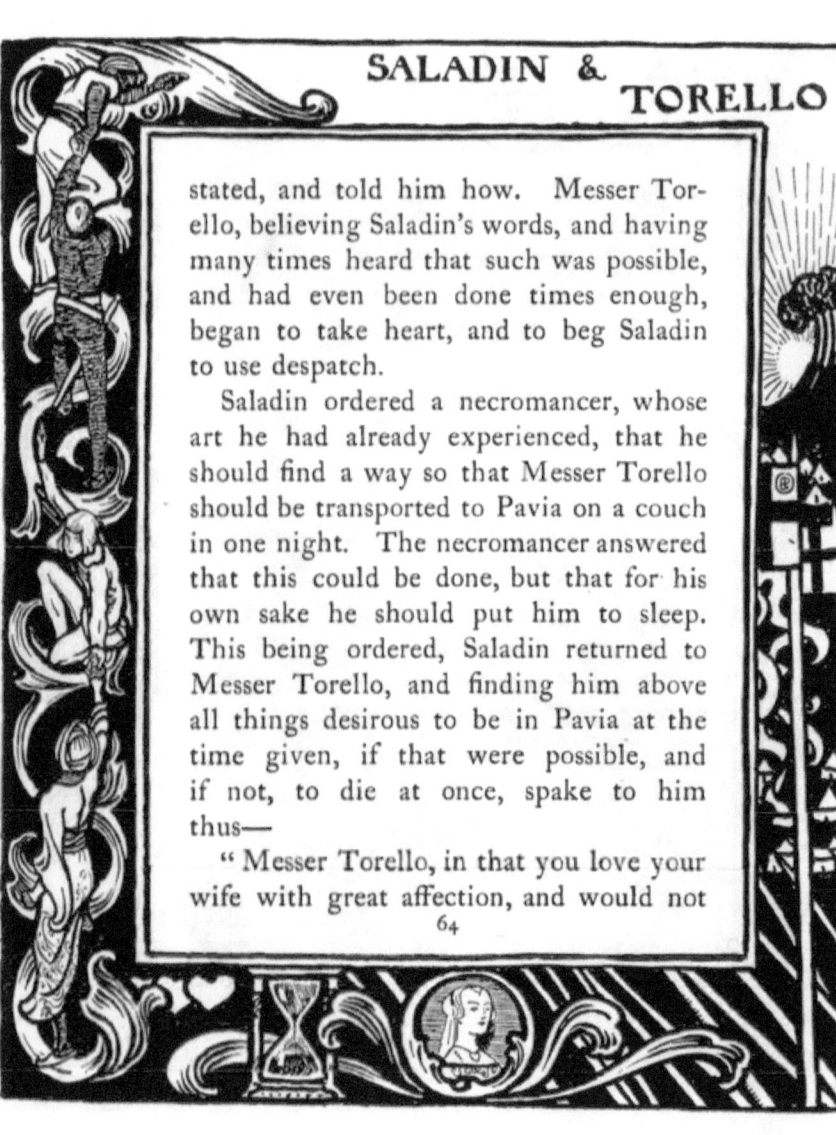

stated, and told him how. Messer Torello, believing Saladin's words, and having
many times heard that such was possible,
and had even been done times enough,
began to take heart, and to beg Saladin
to use despatch.

Saladin ordered a necromancer, whose
art he had already experienced, that he
should find a way so that Messer Torello
should be transported to Pavia on a couch
in one night. The necromancer answered
that this could be done, but that for his
own sake he should put him to sleep.
This being ordered, Saladin returned to
Messer Torello, and finding him above
all things desirous to be in Pavia at the
time given, if that were possible, and
if not, to die at once, spake to him
thus—

"Messer Torello, in that you love your
wife with great affection, and would not

64

that she become another's, God knows
that I in no way blame you therefor,
since of all the women I have chanced to
see, she it is whose manners, bearing, and
character—let alone her beauty, which is
but a short-lived flower—appear to me
most worthy to be praised and held dear.
It would have been most pleasant to me,
since good fortune had brought you to
me, that for the time that you and I
might live, we might have been together,
equal lords in the government of the
kingdom which I hold; but since that
cannot be granted to me by God, since it
has befallen you to be minded either to
die or to return at the stated time to
Pavia, I should have desired to have
known it in time, so that I could have
caused you to be carried to her house
with as much honour, grandeur, and
escort, as your worth deserves; but since

that cannot be granted to me, and you desire to be there at once, I will send you thither as I can, in the way in which I have told you."

Then said Messer Torello to him, " My lord, apart from your words, your deeds have sufficiently proven unto me your goodwill, which surely was never merited by me in so high a degree ; so that I should live and die assured most certainly of what you have just said, even if you had not said it. But since I am thus determined on departure, I pray you that what you have spoken of doing may be done quickly, since to-morrow is the last day that I can be expected."

Saladin said that this should be done without fail, and the following day, intending to send him away the same night, he caused to be made, in a lofty ante-chamber, a goodly and richly-bedecked

66

bed of mattresses, all according to the usage of the Saracens, of velvet and cloth of gold, and laid above it a counterpane bedight with certain designs in pearls of great size and stones of precious value, which were after reckoned as a priceless treasure, besides two pillows suitable for a bed thus decorated. This done, he caused Messer Torello, who was already recovered, to be robed in Saracen-wise, in a garment the richest and most goodly which had ever been seen by any one, while around his head he caused to be wrapped one of his fullest turbans.

The hour being already late, Saladin, with many of his barons, betook himself to the chamber where Messer Torello already was, and placing himself by his side, began to speak to him, almost in tears—

"Messer Torello, the hour which is

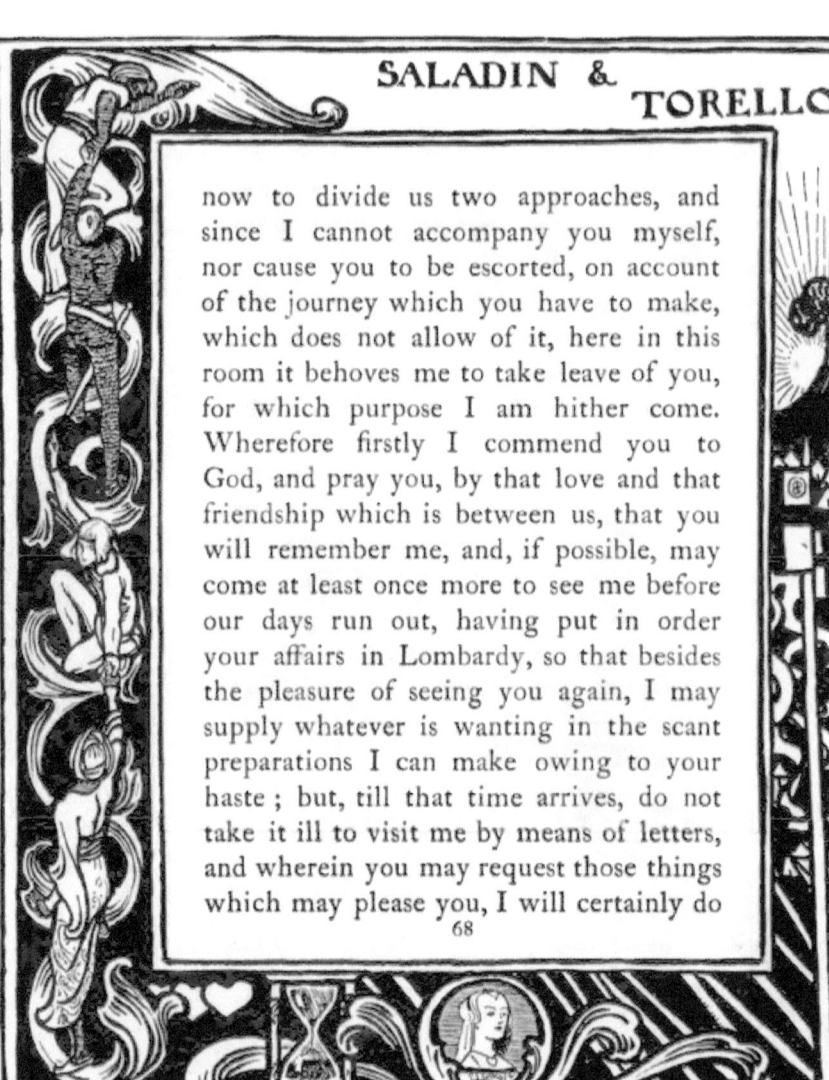

now to divide us two approaches, and
since I cannot accompany you myself,
nor cause you to be escorted, on account
of the journey which you have to make,
which does not allow of it, here in this
room it behoves me to take leave of you,
for which purpose I am hither come.
Wherefore firstly I commend you to
God, and pray you, by that love and that
friendship which is between us, that you
will remember me, and, if possible, may
come at least once more to see me before
our days run out, having put in order
your affairs in Lombardy, so that besides
the pleasure of seeing you again, I may
supply whatever is wanting in the scant
preparations I can make owing to your
haste ; but, till that time arrives, do not
take it ill to visit me by means of letters,
and wherein you may request those things
which may please you, I will certainly do

68

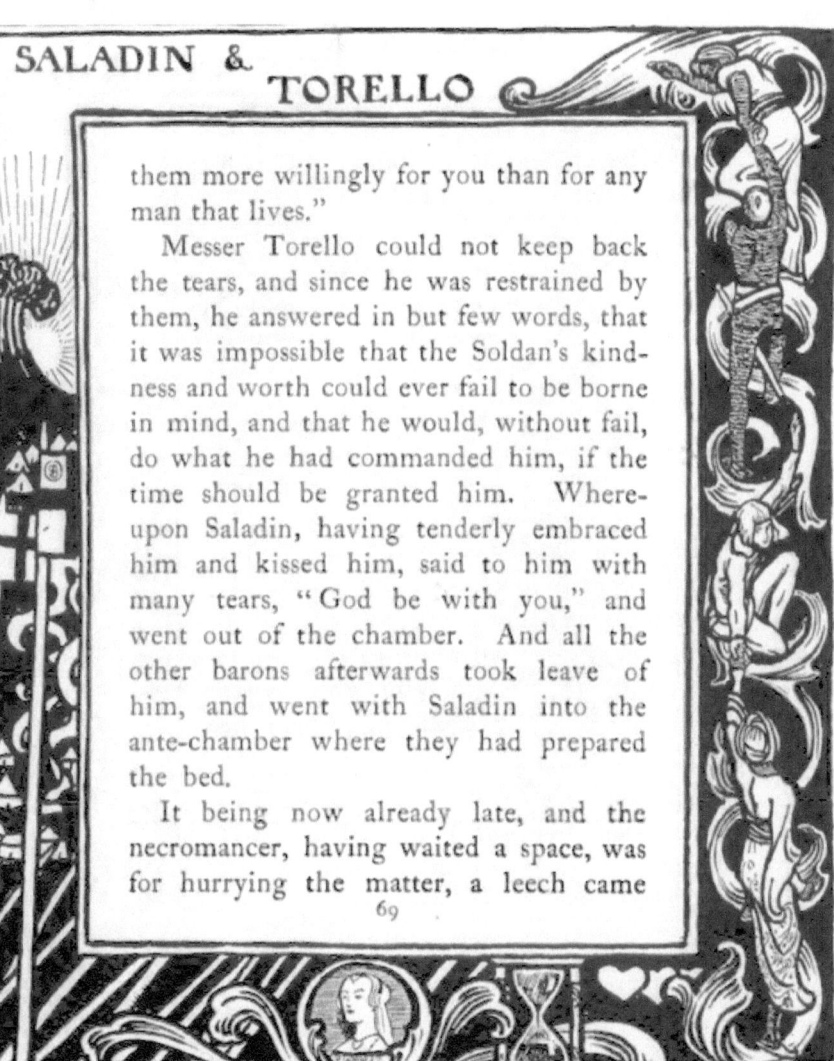

them more willingly for you than for any man that lives."

Messer Torello could not keep back the tears, and since he was restrained by them, he answered in but few words, that it was impossible that the Soldan's kindness and worth could ever fail to be borne in mind, and that he would, without fail, do what he had commanded him, if the time should be granted him. Whereupon Saladin, having tenderly embraced him and kissed him, said to him with many tears, "God be with you," and went out of the chamber. And all the other barons afterwards took leave of him, and went with Saladin into the ante-chamber where they had prepared the bed.

It being now already late, and the necromancer, having waited a space, was for hurrying the matter, a leech came with a beverage, and making show that he was giving it to him to strengthen him, made him drink thereof; nor was it long before he fell into sleep. And while asleep, he was carried by Saladin's commands to his goodly bed, upon which he had placed a large and beautiful crown of great value, with an inscription clearly showing that it was sent from Saladin to Messer Torello's lady. Afterwards he put upon Torello's finger a ring, upon which was fixed a carbuncle so bright that it seemed to be a living torch, and the value of it could scarcely be estimated. Moreover, he caused a sword to be girt about him, the trappings of which were of no slight value. On his breast he caused to be placed a coat of mail, on which were pearls, the like of which had never been seen, with a great quantity of other precious stones. And on either

The bed, with Messer Torello, was taken entirely away

side of him he placed two huge basins
of gold, full of doubloons, with many
strings of pearls, and rings and girdles
and other matters, which to recount
would be too long. This done, once
more he kissed Messer Torello, and then
bade the necromancer make speed, whereupon incontinently, in presence of the
Soldan, the bed, with Messer Torello,
was taken entirely away, while Saladin
and his barons were left talking of him.

Messer Torello was put down, as he
had requested, in the church of San
Pietro in Ciel d'Oro, in Pavia, with all
the above-mentioned jewels and orna-
ments. And while he was still sleeping,
and matins were being rung, the sacristan
entered the church with a light in his
hand, and it happening to him to see
suddenly this rich bed, not alone he
marvelled thereat, but he had the greatest

71

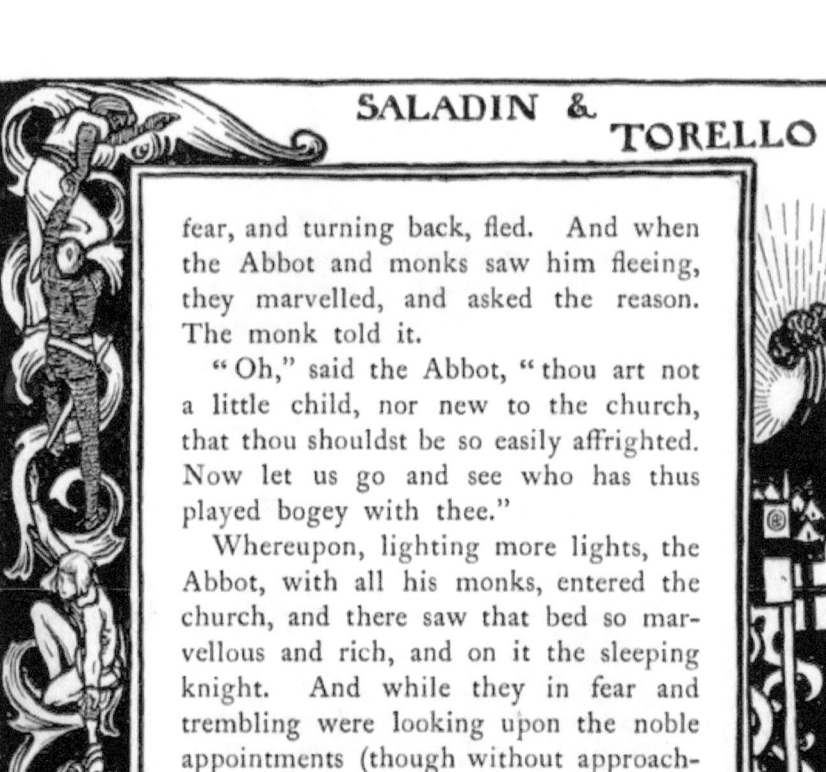

fear, and turning back, fled. And when the Abbot and monks saw him fleeing, they marvelled, and asked the reason. The monk told it.

"Oh," said the Abbot, "thou art not a little child, nor new to the church, that thou shouldst be so easily affrighted. Now let us go and see who has thus played bogey with thee."

Whereupon, lighting more lights, the Abbot, with all his monks, entered the church, and there saw that bed so marvellous and rich, and on it the sleeping knight. And while they in fear and trembling were looking upon the noble appointments (though without approaching the bed), it happened that the effect of the beverage had come to an end, and Messer Torello awoke and gave a great sigh. The monks, when they saw this, and the Abbot with them, being affrighted,

72

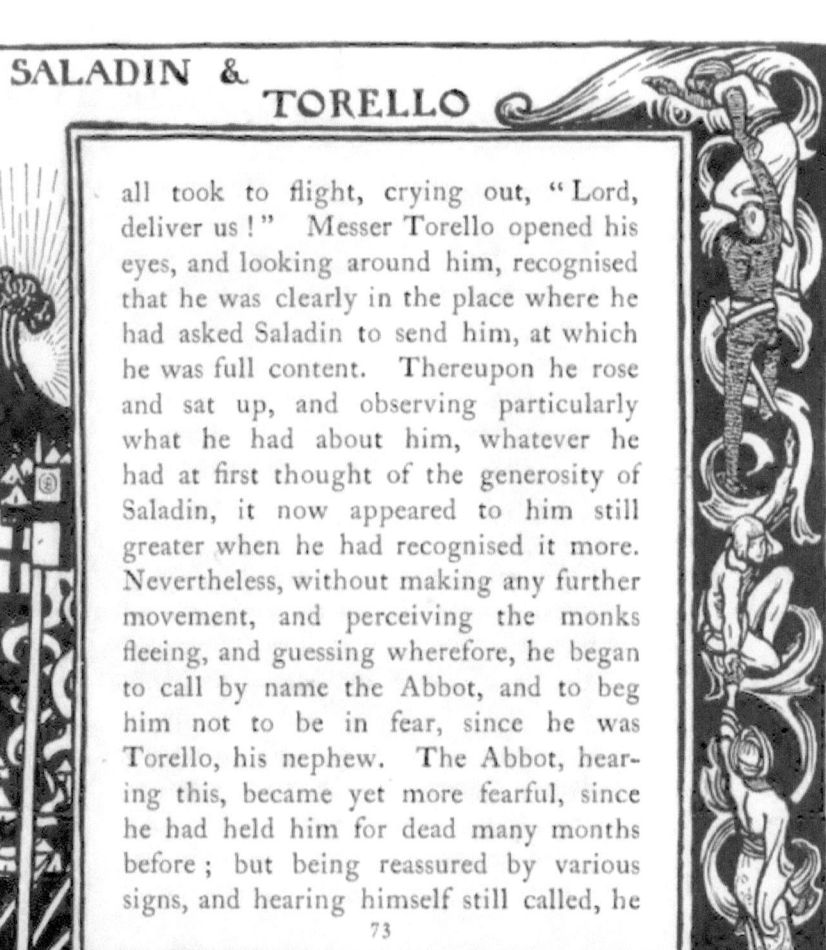

all took to flight, crying out, "Lord, deliver us!" Messer Torello opened his eyes, and looking around him, recognised that he was clearly in the place where he had asked Saladin to send him, at which he was full content. Thereupon he rose and sat up, and observing particularly what he had about him, whatever he had at first thought of the generosity of Saladin, it now appeared to him still greater when he had recognised it more. Nevertheless, without making any further movement, and perceiving the monks fleeing, and guessing wherefore, he began to call by name the Abbot, and to beg him not to be in fear, since he was Torello, his nephew. The Abbot, hearing this, became yet more fearful, since he had held him for dead many months before; but being reassured by various signs, and hearing himself still called, he

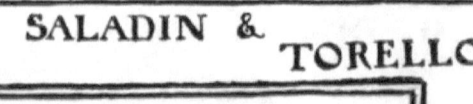

made the sign of the Cross and went to
him.

Then Messer Torello said to him,
"My father, wherefore do ye fear? I
am alive, by God's mercy, and am come
back hither from across the sea."

The Abbot, although he had a long
beard, and was dressed in the Arab mode,
after a while recognised him, and being
all reassured, took him by the hand, and
said—

"My son, thou art welcome." And
went on to say, "Thou must not marvel
at this our fear, since there is not in
all this land a man that does not firmly
believe that thou art dead; so much,
indeed, that I have to tell thee that
Madam Adalieta, thy spouse, overcome
by the prayers and threats of her kinsfolk, and contrary to her own wish, has
been married again, and this very morning

74

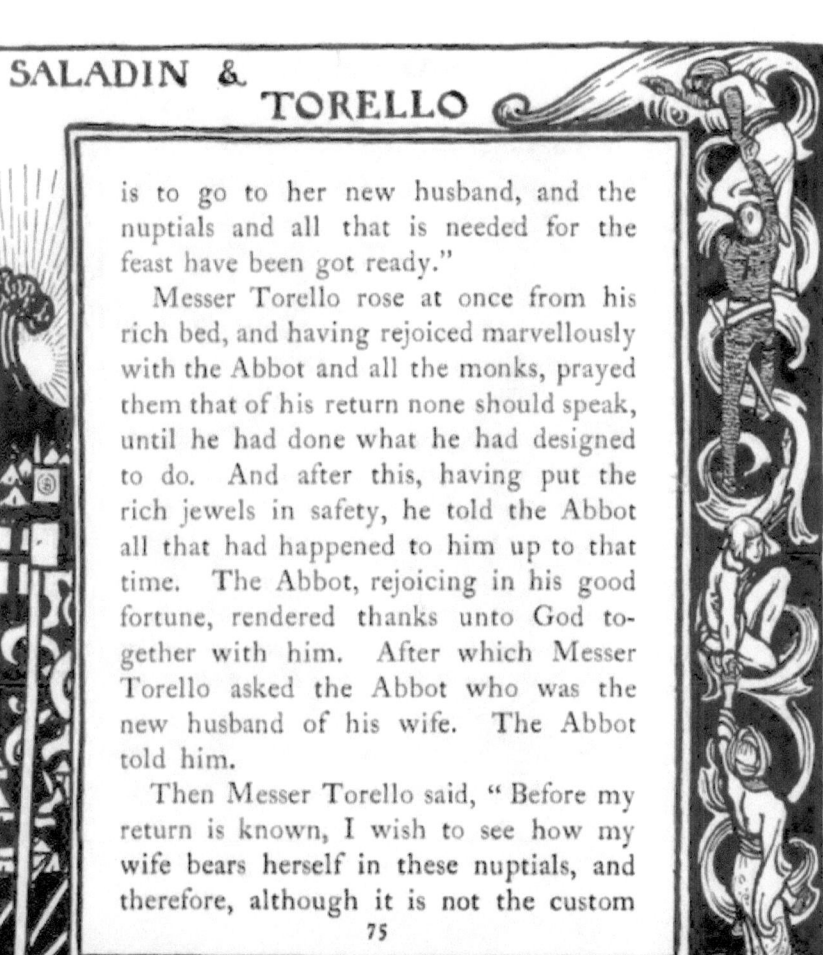

is to go to her new husband, and the nuptials and all that is needed for the feast have been got ready."

Messer Torello rose at once from his rich bed, and having rejoiced marvellously with the Abbot and all the monks, prayed them that of his return none should speak, until he had done what he had designed to do. And after this, having put the rich jewels in safety, he told the Abbot all that had happened to him up to that time. The Abbot, rejoicing in his good fortune, rendered thanks unto God together with him. After which Messer Torello asked the Abbot who was the new husband of his wife. The Abbot told him.

Then Messer Torello said, " Before my return is known, I wish to see how my wife bears herself in these nuptials, and therefore, although it is not the custom

75

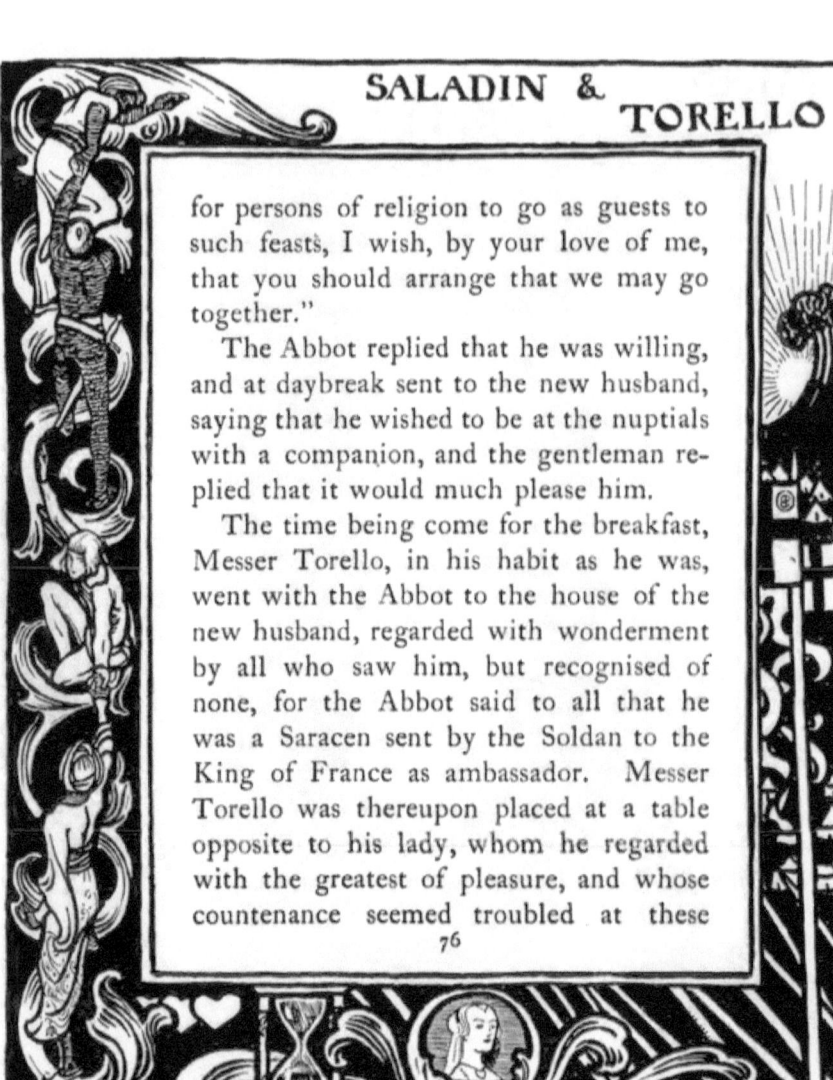

for persons of religion to go as guests to such feasts, I wish, by your love of me, that you should arrange that we may go together."

The Abbot replied that he was willing, and at daybreak sent to the new husband, saying that he wished to be at the nuptials with a companion, and the gentleman replied that it would much please him.

The time being come for the breakfast, Messer Torello, in his habit as he was, went with the Abbot to the house of the new husband, regarded with wonderment by all who saw him, but recognised of none, for the Abbot said to all that he was a Saracen sent by the Soldan to the King of France as ambassador. Messer Torello was thereupon placed at a table opposite to his lady, whom he regarded with the greatest of pleasure, and whose countenance seemed troubled at these

76

nuptials. She, in her turn, looked at him from time to time, not from any recognition that she had of him, since his great beard and foreign dress, and the firm belief she had that he was dead, prevented her. But when the time came that Messer Torello wished to try if she bore him in mind, he took off the ring which had been given to him by his lady when he had parted from her, and calling a young lad who was serving before him, said to him—

"Say on my part to the new bride that in my country it is a custom, when any stranger such as I am here joins in the bridal feast of a new bride such as she is, that she, in sign of holding welcome him who has come to the feast, shall send to him the cup from which she drinks full of wine, and when the stranger has drunk as much as pleases him, she shall

77

drink the rest that is sent back to her in
the cup once more covered."

The lad did his message to the lady,
who, being both wise and well-mannered,
and believing him to be some great per-
sonage, in order to show her pleasure at
his coming, caused a great gilt cup which
she had before her to be first washed and
then filled with wine, and carried to the
gentleman, and thus was it done. Messer
Torello, having put her ring in his mouth,
so managed that as he drank he let it fall
into the cup without any one noticing,
and leaving but little wine in it, covered
the cup again, and sent it to the lady.
She took it and uncovered it, so that she
might carry out that custom, and put it
to her mouth, and then saw the ring, and
without saying anything, looked upon it
somewhat ; and recognising that it was
the ring that she had given to Messer

78

Vaus & Crampton, Sc.

Running to the table where he was seated, she threw herself across
it and embraced him

Torello when he went away, took it, and looked fixedly at him whom she had thought to be a stranger. And recognising him, she became as if distraught, and throwing the table she had before her to the ground, called out, "This is my lord; this is in very sooth Messer Torello!" And running to the table where he was seated, without having regard to her clothes, or to anything that was on the table, she threw herself across it as far as she could, and embraced him closely, nor could she be taken from his neck by deed or word of any one that was there, until she was told by Messer Torello that she should contain herself somewhat, since there would be time enough later on for her to embrace him.

Thereupon she rose up, and the nuptials by this time being all disturbed—though in as joyful a manner as could be—by the

79

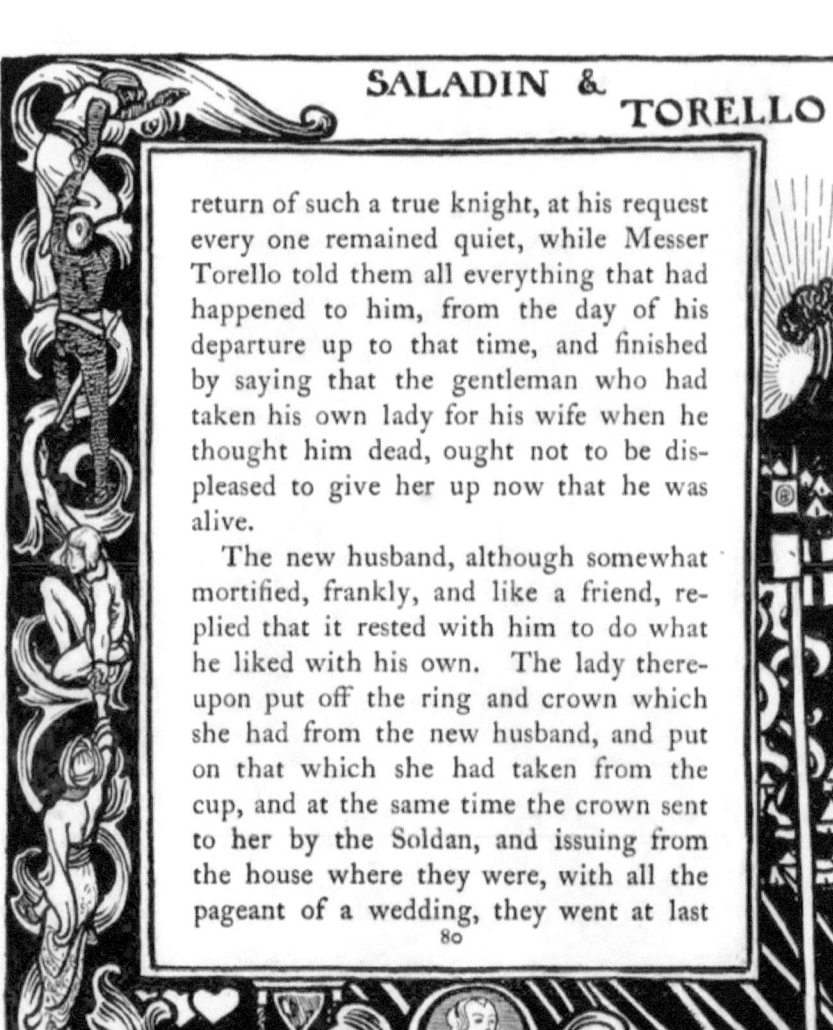

return of such a true knight, at his request
every one remained quiet, while Messer
Torello told them all everything that had
happened to him, from the day of his
departure up to that time, and finished
by saying that the gentleman who had
taken his own lady for his wife when he
thought him dead, ought not to be dis-
pleased to give her up now that he was
alive.

The new husband, although somewhat
mortified, frankly, and like a friend, replied that it rested with him to do what
he liked with his own. The lady thereupon put off the ring and crown which
she had from the new husband, and put
on that which she had taken from the
cup, and at the same time the crown sent
to her by the Soldan, and issuing from
the house where they were, with all the
pageant of a wedding, they went at last

to the house of Messer Torello, and there
he rejoiced by a long and joyful feast his
disconsolate friends and kinsmen, and all
the citizens, who looked upon his return
as a miracle.

Messer Torello then gave of his jewels
to him that had had the expense of the
nuptials, and to the Abbot, and to many
others, and informed Saladin by more
than one message of his happy return to
his own country, though still reckoning
himself his friend and servant, and he
lived many years more with his worthy
lady, using yet more hospitality than
heretofore. Such then was the end of
the troubles of Messer Torello, and of
his dear lady, and the guerdon of their
ready and pleasant courtesy. Many there
are that try to do likewise, since they
have the wherewithal, but do it so badly
that they cause those to whom they extend

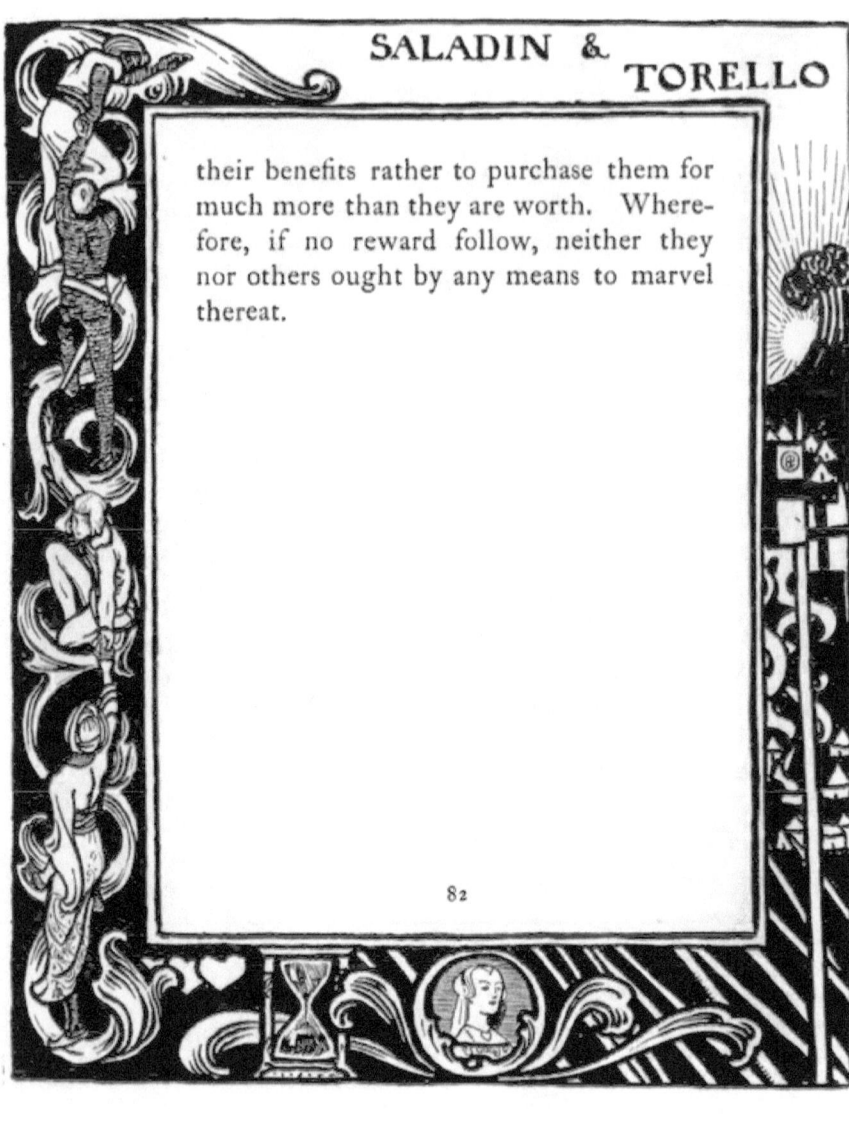

their benefits rather to purchase them for much more than they are worth. Wherefore, if no reward follow, neither they nor others ought by any means to marvel thereat.

Here endeth

the Tale of

Saladin and Torello

Here beginneth
the Tale of
Sir Federigo's Hawk

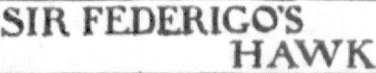

SOME time ago, there was in Florence a young man named Federigo, son of Messer Filippo Alberighi, who was in deeds of arms and in courtesy distinguished above any other squire in Tuscany. Now he, as happens with most gentlemen, fell in love, and with a lady named Monna Giovanna, who was in her time held to be among the most beautiful and graceful women in Florence. And to the end that he might gain her love, he fought in tilts and tourneys, gave entertainments, and made presents, expending his means without the slightest moderation. But she, not less pure than beautiful, cared naught for the things which he did for her, nor for him that did them. Spending therefore right and left with all his might, and acquiring nothing, as easily happens, Federigo's riches vanished and he became

87

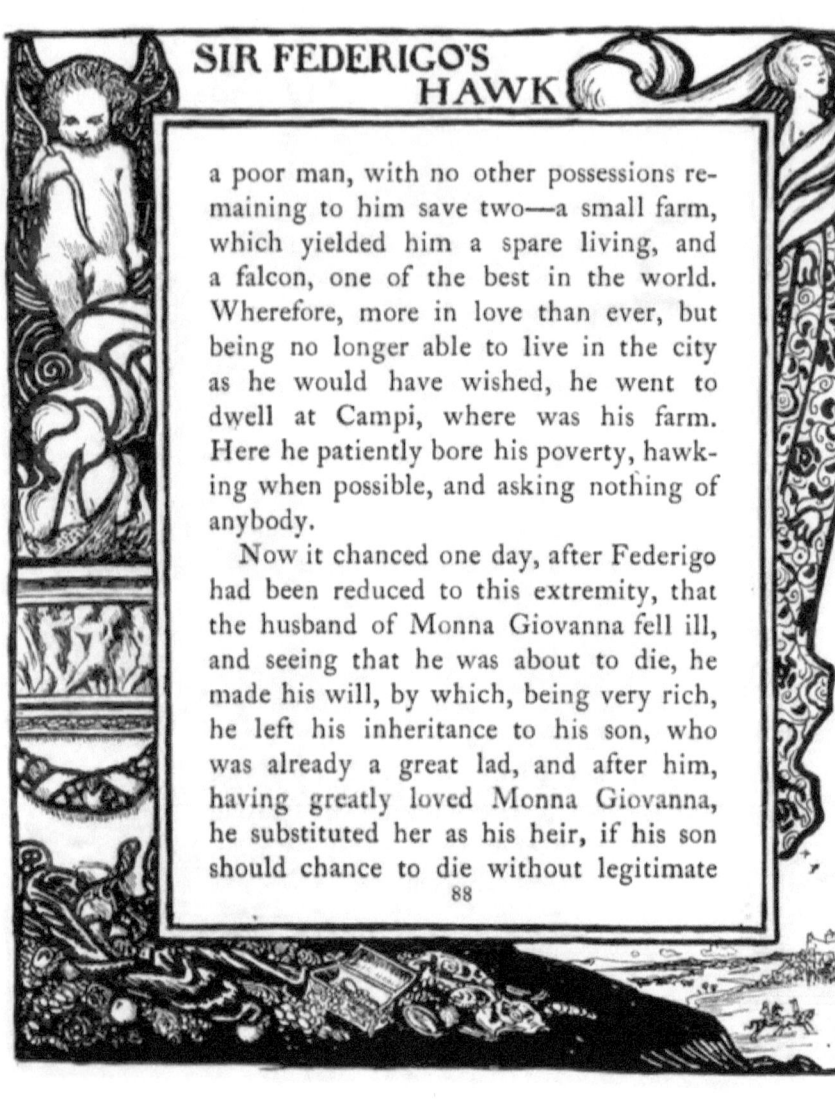

a poor man, with no other possessions remaining to him save two—a small farm,
which yielded him a spare living, and
a falcon, one of the best in the world.
Wherefore, more in love than ever, but
being no longer able to live in the city
as he would have wished, he went to
dwell at Campi, where was his farm.
Here he patiently bore his poverty, hawking when possible, and asking nothing of
anybody.

Now it chanced one day, after Federigo
had been reduced to this extremity, that
the husband of Monna Giovanna fell ill,
and seeing that he was about to die, he
made his will, by which, being very rich,
he left his inheritance to his son, who
was already a great lad, and after him,
having greatly loved Monna Giovanna,
he substituted her as his heir, if his son
should chance to die without legitimate

88

Vaus & Crampton, Sc.

Having many times seen the flight of Federigo's falcon, he desired

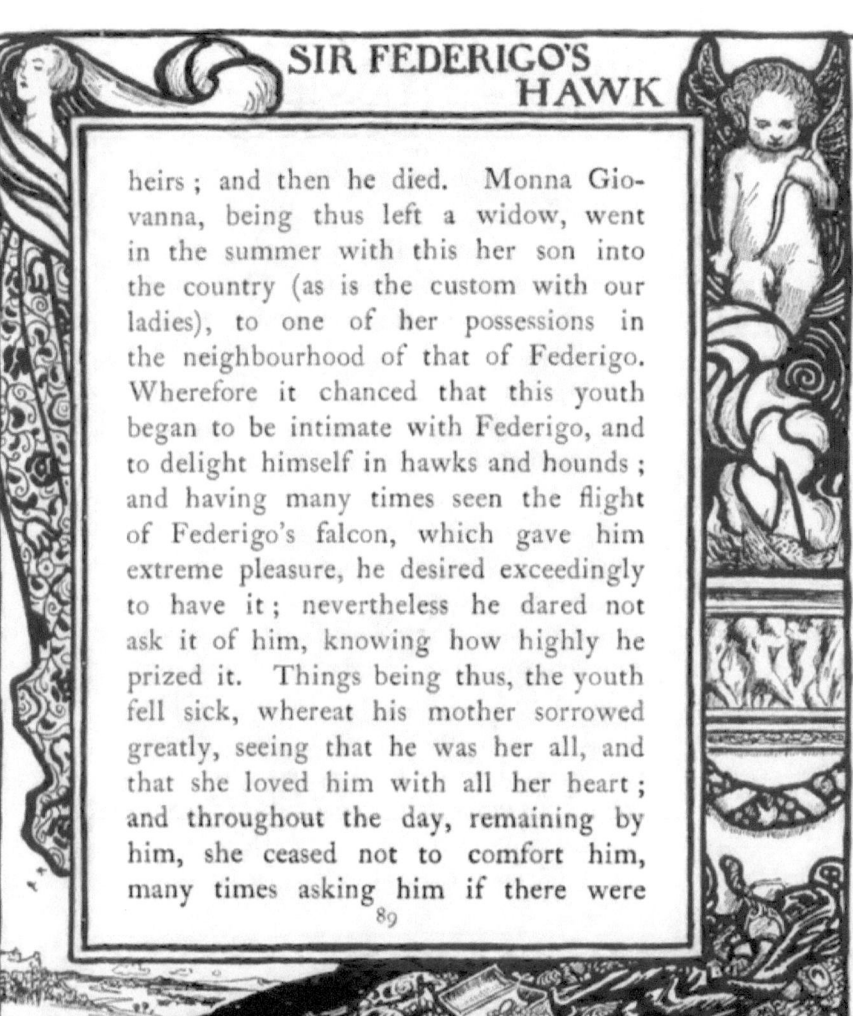

heirs ; and then he died. Monna Giovanna, being thus left a widow, went
in the summer with this her son into
the country (as is the custom with our
ladies), to one of her possessions in
the neighbourhood of that of Federigo.
Wherefore it chanced that this youth
began to be intimate with Federigo, and
to delight himself in hawks and hounds ;
and having many times seen the flight
of Federigo's falcon, which gave him
extreme pleasure, he desired exceedingly
to have it ; nevertheless he dared not
ask it of him, knowing how highly he
prized it. Things being thus, the youth
fell sick, whereat his mother sorrowed
greatly, seeing that he was her all, and
that she loved him with all her heart ;
and throughout the day, remaining by
him, she ceased not to comfort him,
many times asking him if there were

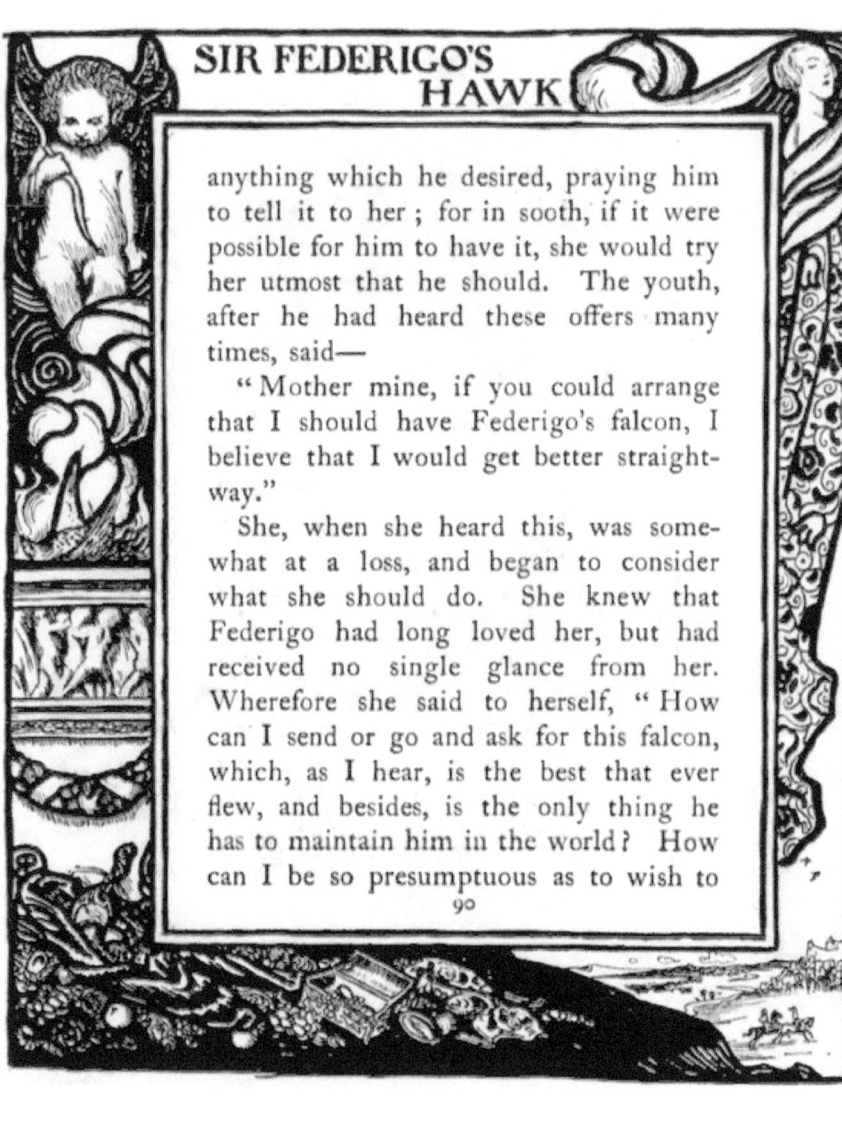

anything which he desired, praying him
to tell it to her ; for in sooth, if it were
possible for him to have it, she would try
her utmost that he should. The youth,
after he had heard these offers many
times, said—

"Mother mine, if you could arrange
that I should have Federigo's falcon, I
believe that I would get better straightway."

She, when she heard this, was somewhat at a loss, and began to consider
what she should do. She knew that
Federigo had long loved her, but had
received no single glance from her.
Wherefore she said to herself, "How
can I send or go and ask for this falcon,
which, as I hear, is the best that ever
flew, and besides, is the only thing he
has to maintain him in the world? How
can I be so presumptuous as to wish to

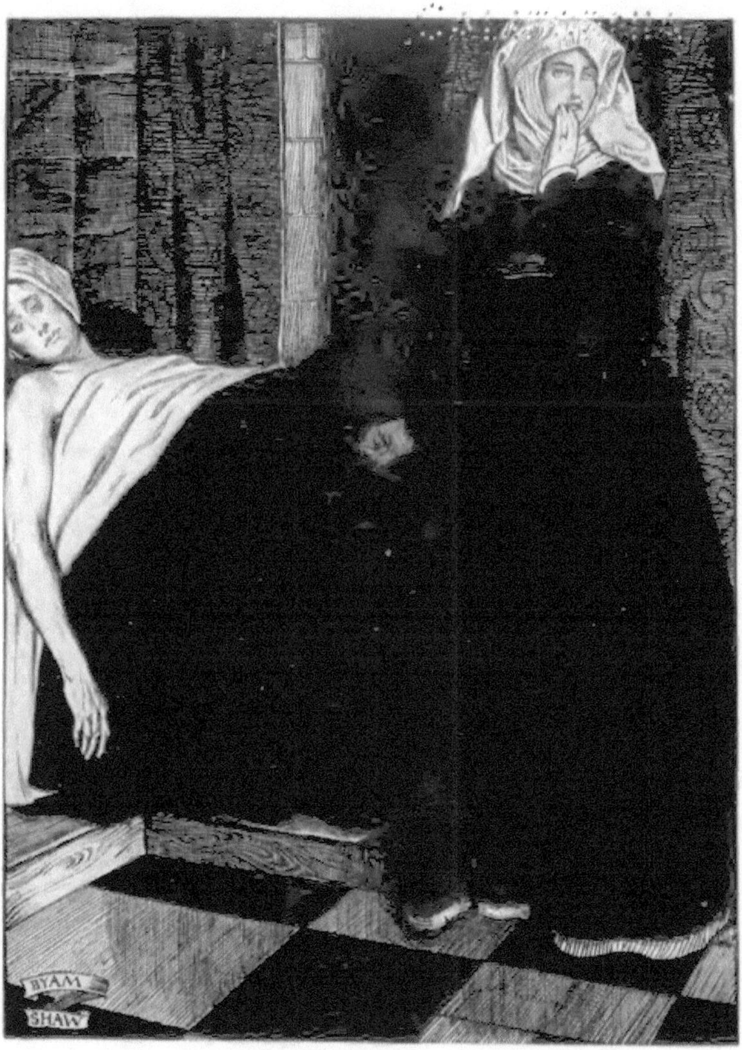

Vaus & Crampton, Sc *P. 90*

She, when she heard this, was somewhat at a loss

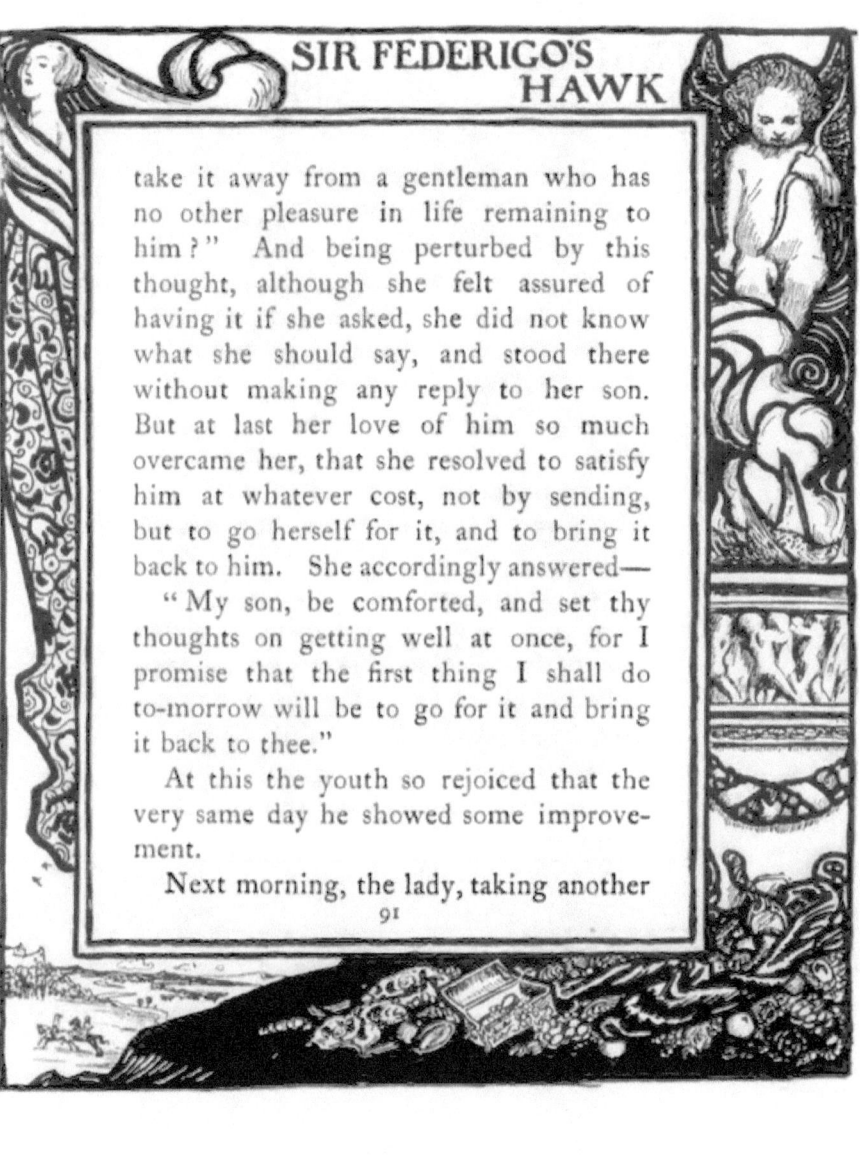

take it away from a gentleman who has
no other pleasure in life remaining to
him?" And being perturbed by this
thought, although she felt assured of
having it if she asked, she did not know
what she should say, and stood there
without making any reply to her son.
But at last her love of him so much
overcame her, that she resolved to satisfy
him at whatever cost, not by sending,
but to go herself for it, and to bring it
back to him. She accordingly answered—

"My son, be comforted, and set thy
thoughts on getting well at once, for I
promise that the first thing I shall do
to-morrow will be to go for it and bring
it back to thee."

At this the youth so rejoiced that the
very same day he showed some improve-
ment.

Next morning, the lady, taking another

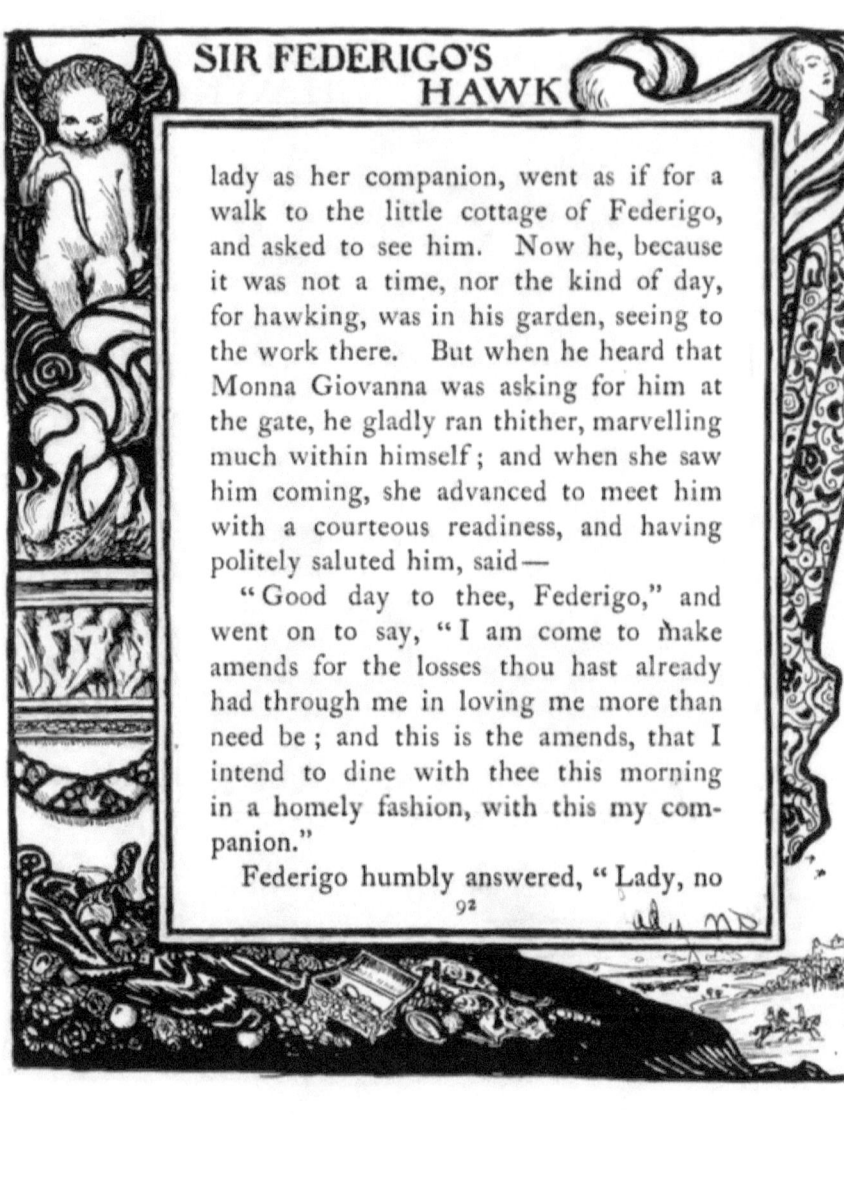

lady as her companion, went as if for a
walk to the little cottage of Federigo,
and asked to see him. Now he, because
it was not a time, nor the kind of day,
for hawking, was in his garden, seeing to
the work there. But when he heard that
Monna Giovanna was asking for him at
the gate, he gladly ran thither, marvelling
much within himself; and when she saw
him coming, she advanced to meet him
with a courteous readiness, and having
politely saluted him, said—

"Good day to thee, Federigo," and
went on to say, "I am come to make
amends for the losses thou hast already
had through me in loving me more than
need be; and this is the amends, that I
intend to dine with thee this morning
in a homely fashion, with this my companion."

Federigo humbly answered, "Lady, no

92

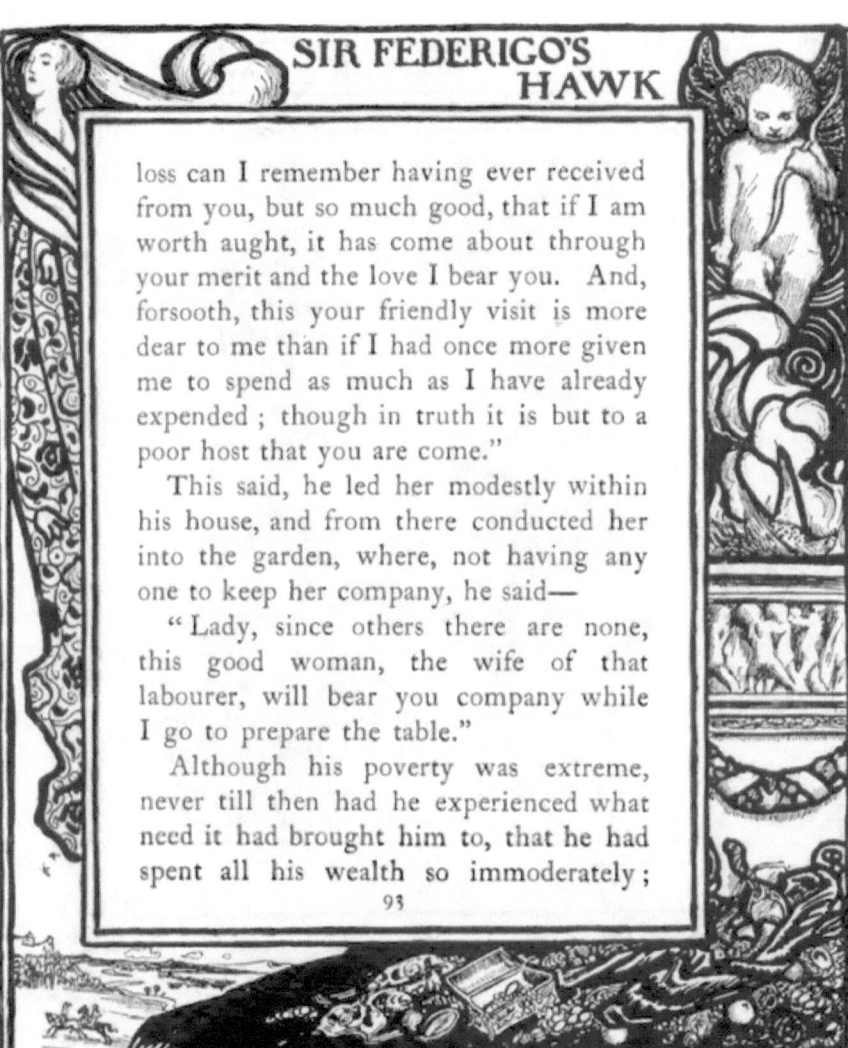

loss can I remember having ever received from you, but so much good, that if I am worth aught, it has come about through your merit and the love I bear you. And, forsooth, this your friendly visit is more dear to me than if I had once more given me to spend as much as I have already expended ; though in truth it is but to a poor host that you are come."

This said, he led her modestly within his house, and from there conducted her into the garden, where, not having any one to keep her company, he said—

"Lady, since others there are none, this good woman, the wife of that labourer, will bear you company while I go to prepare the table."

Although his poverty was extreme, never till then had he experienced what need it had brought him to, that he had spent all his wealth so immoderately ;

93

but this morning, finding no single thing by which he could honour the lady for love of whom he had done honour to innumerable men, he was nigh distraught, and full of anxiety he ran hither and thither like a man beside himself, cursing his evil fortune. At length, having no money, and finding no pledge, the hour being late, and his desire great to do honour in some way to the noble lady, and not wishing to make appeal to any one (not even to his own labourer), he cast his eyes upon his good falcon, which stood upon its perch in its hutch, and having no other resource, he took it and found it fat, and it seemed to him a worthy viand for such a lady ; and incontinently, without more thought, he twisted its neck, and ordered the kitchen wench to pluck it and put it on the spit and roast it carefully, while he prepared

P. 95

Incontinently, without more thought, he twisted its neck

the table with napery most white, for of
such he still had some store.   Then returning with joyful visage to the lady in
his garden, he told her that the repast
—such as it was—was ready for her.
Whereupon the lady, with her companion, arose and seated herself at table,
and without knowing what she was
tasting, she ate the good falcon, while
Federigo served her with the utmost
respect.

After they had risen from table, and
had spent some time in pleasant conversation, it seemed to the lady time to say
that for which she had come, and turning
courteously towards Federigo, she began
to speak.

"Federigo, if thou hast in memory thy
past life, and my determination, which
peradventure thou hast considered hard-
ness and cruelty, I doubt not that thou

95

wilt marvel at my presumption when
thou hast learnt why chiefly I am come ;
but if thou hadst or hadst had children,
thou wouldst know what may be the
power of the love we bear them, and I
am certain thou wouldst hold me in part
excused ; however, thou hast none, while
I, that have but one, have not been able
to escape the laws common to other
mothers, which I find myself forced to
obey. I thus find myself obliged against
my wish, and against all reason and right,
to ask of thee as a gift that which I
know is to thee most dearly dear, and
with reason, since there is no other
pleasure or diversion or consolation left
thee in the extreme of thy ill fortune.
This gift is that falcon of thine, to which
my little son is so strongly attached, that
if I do not bear it back to him, I fear he
will not be able to bear it, such is the

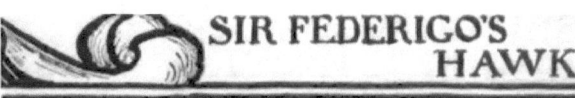

weakness in which he now is, so that through no other thing than this I shall lose him. Therefore I pray thee, not for the love which thou bearest me, as to which thou art in no way obliged to me, but by thy very generosity, which thou hast displayed in courteous usage more than any other man, that thou mayest be pleased to give it to him, so that by that gift I may say that I have received the life of my little son, and through that will be always under obligation to thee."

Federigo, when he heard what the lady demanded, and feeling that he could not help her, because he had given it to her to eat, began in her presence to weep, without having any word to reply to her; the which weeping the lady at first thought came more than aught else from grief at having to part from his good

falcon, and was as much as to say that
he was not willing ; but nevertheless she
contained herself, and waited till he had
ended his weeping for Federigo's reply,
who thus spake to her—

"Lady, ever since that it pleased God
that I should place my love in you, in
many things enough has Fortune proved
herself my enemy, and much have I
grieved thereat ; but all such things are
as naught in view of that which she has
done to me at present, for which I can
never have peace with her henceforth :
to think that you have come to my poor
house here (where, while I was rich,
you would not deign to come), and have
asked from me a slight gift, and then
Fortune has so brought it about that I
cannot give it ! And why I cannot I will
briefly tell. When I heard that you, in
your condescension, desired to dine with

98

me, having regard to your excellency and
your merit, I considered it a right worthy
and fitting thing that I should honour
you with the richest viand within my
power—richer than anything else which
is generally granted to other persons.
Wherefore, bethinking myself of the
falcon which you have just asked of me,
and of his goodness, I considered him
worthy food for you, and this morn you
have had him roasted on a platter.   And
I would have thought him thus best dis-
posed of, but that now I see that you
desire him in another fashion, which
gives me so great a grief, in that I
cannot serve you, that I cannot think
evermore to have peace."

This said, he cast before her in witness
the wings and feet and beak.   And when
the lady heard and saw this, at first she
blamed him for having killed such a

falcon to give it to eat to a woman, but then within herself she honoured the greatness of his soul, which poverty was not able to abate.

Being thus without hope of having the falcon and of securing the health of her son, all melancholy she departed, and returned to him; and he, either through grief at not having the falcon, or through the weakness to which he had been brought, passed from this life after a few days, to the great grief of his mother.

Now she, although she remained for some time full of tears and grief, being of great riches and still young, was many times pressed by her brothers to marry again. She, however, did not wish this, but seeing them insist, and remembering the merit of Federigo and his latest piece of generosity, in that he had killed such a falcon to do her honour, she said to her brothers—

" I would prefer, an you please, to remain as I am, but since it rather pleases you more that I should take a husband, in sooth I will take none other unless I have Federigo degli Alberighi."

At which her brothers, making mock of her, said, " Fool ! what is it that thou sayest ? How canst thou desire him, that has not a thing in the world ? "

And she said to them, " My brothers, I know well that it is as you say, but I prefer to have a man without riches, than to have riches with an apology for a man."

Her brothers, hearing such was her mood, and knowing well that Federigo—however poor he was—was such an one as she wanted, gave her to him with all her riches ; and he, seeing that he had for wife the lady whom he loved so much, and, besides this, becoming rich again through her, ended his years in gladness by her side, taking better care of his fortune.

Here endeth

the Tale of

Sir Federigo's Hawk

Here beginneth
the Tale of
Isabella

BYAM·SHAW

Vaus & Crampton, Sc. *p. 107*

No great time passed before that came to pass which both most desired

ISABELLA

AT a time there lived in Messina three brothers, still youths, but yet merchants, and left passing rich men by the death of their father, who was from San Gimignano. Now they had one only sister, named Isabella, a damsel both beautiful and well bred, whom they had not yet married, for that no occasion had arisen. These three brothers also had in one of their factories a Pisan youth named Lorenzo, who guided and ruled all their affairs ; and it came to pass that, he being very handsome in person and charming in manner, Isabella, after she had seen him many a time and oft, began to take a strange pleasure in him, the said Lorenzo having likewise left all his other loves and begun to fix his mind on her. And the matter went so far that, as they pleased one another equally, no great time passed

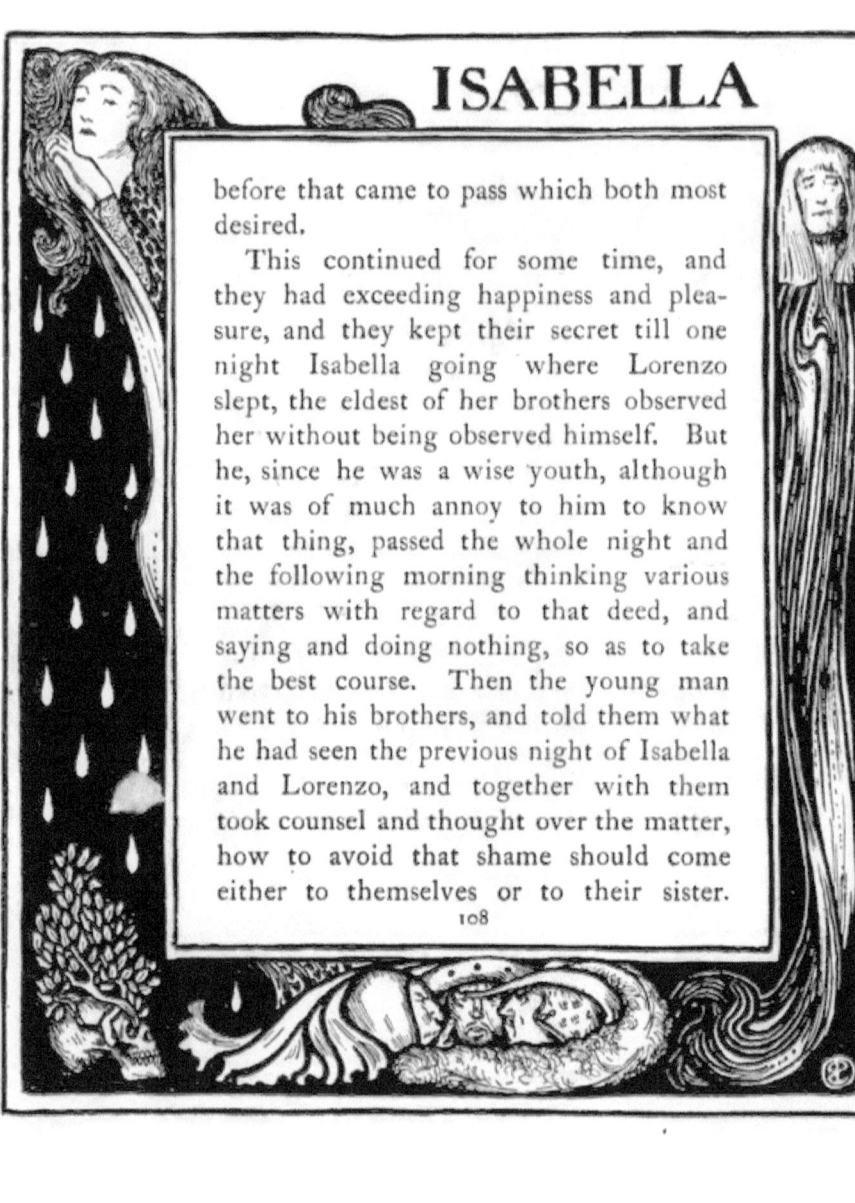

before that came to pass which both most
desired.

This continued for some time, and
they had exceeding happiness and pleasure, and they kept their secret till one
night Isabella going where Lorenzo
slept, the eldest of her brothers observed
her without being observed himself. But
he, since he was a wise youth, although
it was of much annoy to him to know
that thing, passed the whole night and
the following morning thinking various
matters with regard to that deed, and
saying and doing nothing, so as to take
the best course. Then the young man
went to his brothers, and told them what
he had seen the previous night of Isabella
and Lorenzo, and together with them
took counsel and thought over the matter,
how to avoid that shame should come
either to themselves or to their sister.

Vaus & Crampton, Sc.   P. 105

Then the young man, together with his brothers, took counsel

ISABELLA

And they determined to pass over the
matter in silence, and to conceal from all
that they had seen or known of anything,
to the end that, when the time came
when they could take vengeance without
loss or damage to themselves, it would
come about better if they could take him
out of sight.   And remaining of that
mind, they continued laughing and joking
with Lorenzo as of old, till the time came
when, making a semblance of going outside the city for their pleasure, they took
with them Lorenzo.   And when they
arrived in a remote and lonesome spot,
seeing their opportunity when Lorenzo
was off his guard, they killed him, and
buried him in such manner that no
person could come across him, and
turning back to Messina, pretended that
they had sent him for their needs to
another place, which could the more

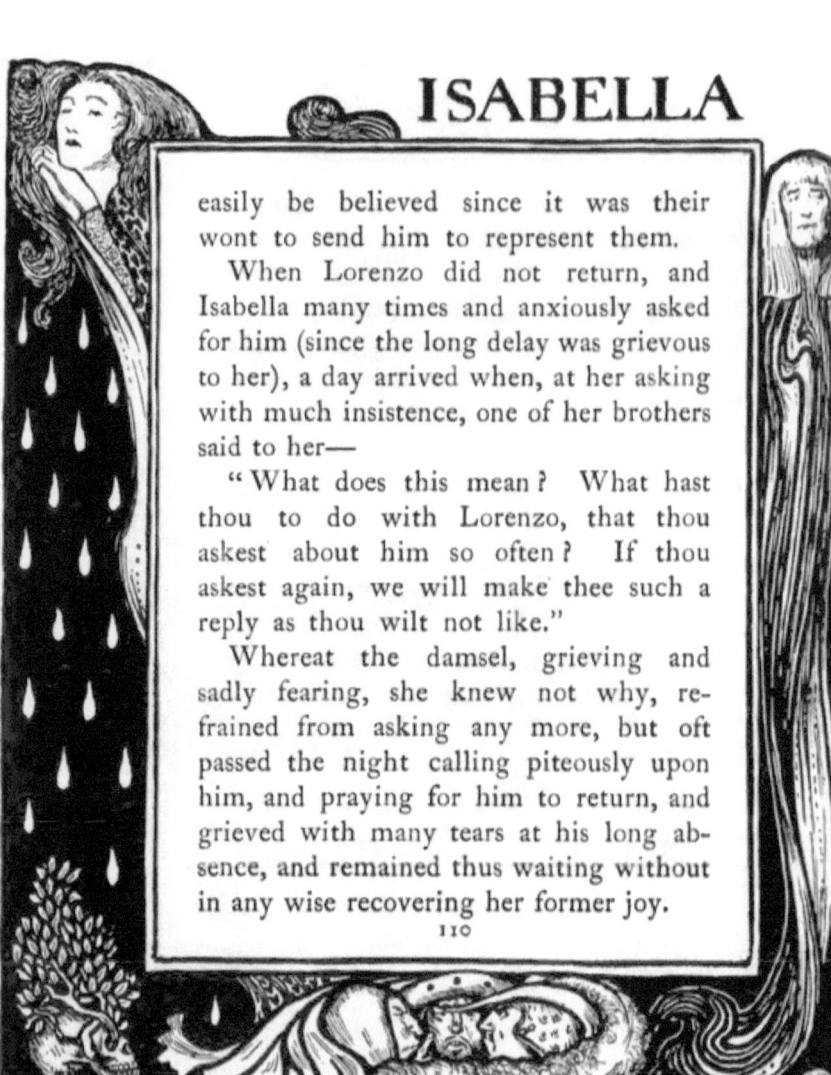

easily be believed since it was their wont to send him to represent them.

When Lorenzo did not return, and Isabella many times and anxiously asked for him (since the long delay was grievous to her), a day arrived when, at her asking with much insistence, one of her brothers said to her—

"What does this mean? What hast thou to do with Lorenzo, that thou askest about him so often? If thou askest again, we will make thee such a reply as thou wilt not like."

Whereat the damsel, grieving and sadly fearing, she knew not why, refrained from asking any more, but oft passed the night calling piteously upon him, and praying for him to return, and grieved with many tears at his long absence, and remained thus waiting without in any wise recovering her former joy.

There appeared to her Lorenzo in a dream, pale and distraught

BELLA

Now there came one night when, having thus greatly grieved for her Lorenzo, that he did not return, she bewept herself asleep at last, and there appeared to her Lorenzo in a dream, pale and distraught, and with all his garments rent and decayed, and it seemed to her that he said—

"Ah, Isabella, thou dost nothing but cry out and sadden thyself at my long absence, and accusest me bitterly with thy tears. Know then, therefore, that I cannot return any more, because on the last day on which thou sawest me thy brothers killed me."

And then, having pointed out the place where they had buried him, he bade her call upon him no more, for that she would never see him again, and thereupon disappeared.

The damsel woke up, and, believing in

the vision, grieved bitterly ; then rising
up in the morning, and not daring to
say aught to her brothers, she determined
to go to the place pointed out, and to see
if that were true which had appeared to
her in her dream. And having received
leave to go for a stroll into the country
with one of her women, who had been
with her at other times and knew all her
affairs, she went there as quickly as possible, and removing the dead leaves which
were in that place, she digged where the
earth seemed least hard. She had not
digged far ere she found the body of her
poor lover, in no wise wasted or corrupt,
so that she knew that in very deed her
vision was true. Whereat, instead of
lamenting like a sorrowing woman (for
she knew that this was not the place for
tears), she would willingly have taken
the whole body with her, so that it might

112

She wrapped the head in a cloth, and gave it to her maid-servant to carry

ISABELLA

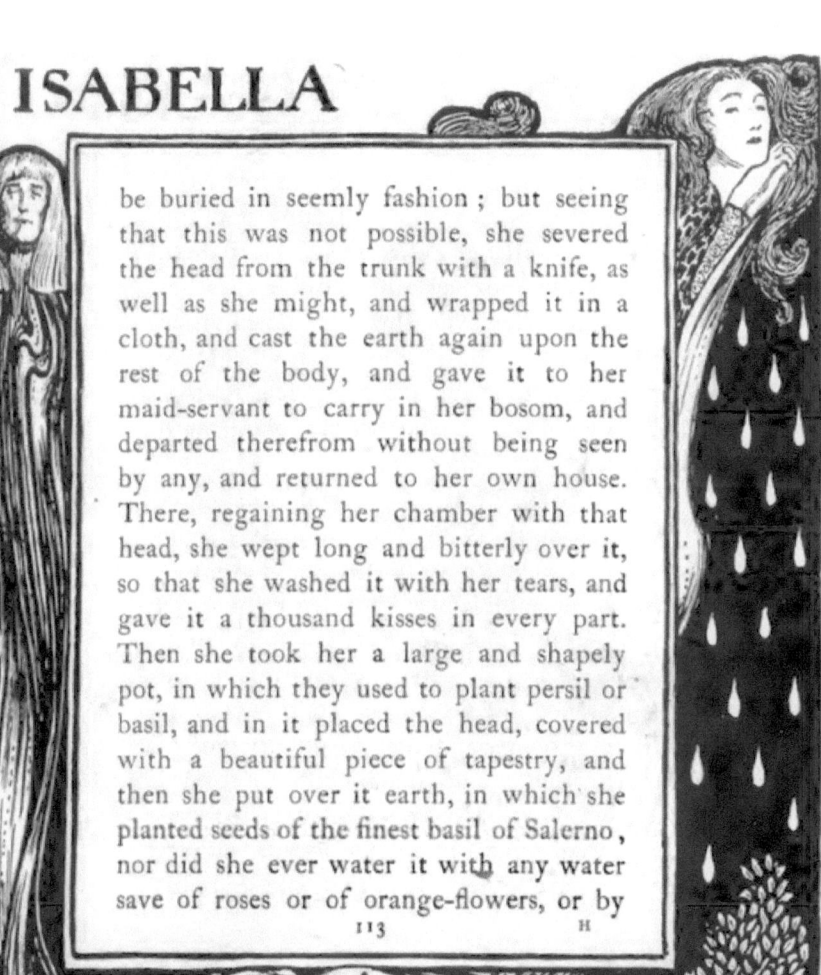

be buried in seemly fashion; but seeing
that this was not possible, she severed
the head from the trunk with a knife, as
well as she might, and wrapped it in a
cloth, and cast the earth again upon the
rest of the body, and gave it to her
maid-servant to carry in her bosom, and
departed therefrom without being seen
by any, and returned to her own house.
There, regaining her chamber with that
head, she wept long and bitterly over it,
so that she washed it with her tears, and
gave it a thousand kisses in every part.
Then she took her a large and shapely
pot, in which they used to plant persil or
basil, and in it placed the head, covered
with a beautiful piece of tapestry, and
then she put over it earth, in which she
planted seeds of the finest basil of Salerno,
nor did she ever water it with any water
save of roses or of orange-flowers, or by

her own tears. And it became her wont to sit always near the self-same pot, and she placed all her desire in it, as if it held her Lorenzo in very deed hidden within it. And whenever she had gazed upon it for a time, she would always begin to weep, and that for a long space, so that she would bathe the whole plant with her tears.

The basil, by this long and continuous care, as well as by the richness of the earth proceeding from the corruption of the head which was within it, became most beautiful, and gave forth a most sweet perfume. As she continued this behaviour, she was observed many times by neighbours, and they spake thereof to her brothers, who had begun to marvel at her wasted beauty, and that her eyes appeared sunk into her head, saying, "We have noted this, that she behaves

ISABELLA

in such and such a manner day after day." And when they heard this, the brothers assured themselves of the fact, and after they had reproved her for some time without success, they let carry away that pot, all in secret. And when she could not find it again, though she had asked for it time after time with great insistence, and it was not given back to her, from her incessant grief and tears she fell ill and did naught else but ask for that pot in her illness. The young men marvelled much at this demand, and desirous of seeing what was within it, removed the earth, and there saw the cloth, and in it the head, still not consumed away, so that they could see from the curly hair that it was the head of Lorenzo, at which they marvelled much, and feared that the matter would come to light. They thereupon buried it again,

and without saying aught, fled with care from Messina, and having given orders how their affairs should be removed thence, betook themselves to Naples. But Isabella did not cease from weeping, nor from asking for her pot again, and in so weeping died. And thus her misfortunate love had its end.

But thereupon, after a time, the matter became manifest to many, and there was one composed a song, which is sung even at the present day, and thus it begins—

" No true follower of our Lord was he
That of my basil bereavèd me."

And thus her misfortunate love had its end

Here endeth
the Tale of
Isabella

Printed by
BALLANTYNE, HANSON & Co.
Edinburgh

www.ingramcontent.com/pod-product-compliance
Lightning Source LLC
Chambersburg PA
CBHW022354020726
47500CB00002B/273